NAGUIB MAHFOUZ

The Seventh Heaven

Naguib Mahfouz was born in Cairo in 1911 and began writing when he was seventeen. A student of philosophy and an avid reader, his works range from reimaginings of ancient myths to subtle commentaries on contemporary Egyptian politics and culture. Over a career that lasted more than five decades, he wrote 33 novels, 13 short story anthologies, numerous plays, and 30 screenplays. Of his many works, most famous is *The Cairo Trilogy*, consisting of *Palace Walk* (1956), *Palace of Desire* (1957), and *Sugar Street* (1957), which focuses on a Cairo family through three generations, from 1917 until 1952. In 1988, he was awarded the Nobel Prize in Literature, the first writer in Arabic to do so. He died in August 2006.

Raymond Stock (translator) is writing a biography of Naguib Mahfouz. He is the translator of Mahfouz's *Voices from the Other World*, *Khufu's Wisdom*, and *The Dreams*.

The following titles by Naguib Mahfouz are
also published by Anchor Books:

The Beggar*
The Thief and the Dogs*
Autumn Quail*
The Beginning and the End
Wedding Song†
Respected Sir†
The Time and the Place and Other Stories
The Search†
Midaq Alley
The Journey of Ibn Fattouma
Miramar
Adrift on the Nile
The Harafish
Arabian Nights and Days
Children of the Alley
Echoes of an Autobiography
The Day the Leader Was Killed
Akhenaten, Dweller in Truth
Voices from the Other World
Rhadopis of Nubia
Khufu's Wisdom

The Cairo Trilogy:
Palace Walk
Palace of Desire
Sugar Street

*†published as omnibus editions

The Seventh Heaven

The Seventh Heaven

Stories of the Supernatural

NAGUIB MAHFOUZ

Selected, Introduced,
and Translated from the Arabic
by Raymond Stock

ANCHOR BOOKS

A DIVISION OF RANDOM HOUSE, INC.

NEW YORK

FIRST ANCHOR BOOKS EDITION, DECEMBER 2006

"The Disturbing Occurrences" appeared in *Harper's Magazine*,
August 2005. "Room No. 12" appeared in *Zoetrope: All-Story*
magazine, Fall 2005. "The Haunted Wood" appeared in *Bookforum,*
December/January 2004/5. "The Rose Garden" appeared in *nest: a
quarterly of interiors* in Winter 1999/2000. "The Reception Hall"
appeared in *Egypt Today*, December 1996. "A Warning from Afar"
appeared in *Bookforum*, December/January 2004/5.

The Cataloging-in-Publication Data for *The Seventh Heaven*
is on file at the Library of Congress.

**Anchor ISBN-10: 0-307-27714-3
Anchor ISBN-13: 978-0-307-27714-5**

www.anchorbooks.com

Printed in the United States of America
10 9 8 7 6 5 4 3 2 1

Contents

Translator's Introduction

On Pembroke Road look out for my ghost
Dishevelled with shoes untied,
Playing through the railings with little children
Whose children have long since died.

— Patrick Kavanagh[1]

Egyptian writer Naguib Mahfouz, who in 1988 became the first Arab Nobel laureate in literature, is justifiably known as one of the greatest realist writers of the last century. But he is equally a master of the bizarre, the supernatural, even the macabre.

To be sure, Mahfouz's *oeuvre*, encompassing some sixty books covering virtually every style and genre of fiction, is both vast and immensely varied. Best known for straightforward stories of life in his native city, such as his famous *Cairo Trilogy (Palace Walk, Palace of Desire,* and *Sugar Street)*, so accurately does he capture the ways of the poor that it is said you can smell the "popular quarters" on the page. Yet in the same works and many others, he is just as adept at portraying the wealthy and the middle class, both women and men.

This same versatility extends to time and place as well: some of his earliest stories are highly readable (though for long, oddly underrated), increasingly allegorical romances set in his country's rich pharaonic past. His first three "historical" novels, *Khufu's Wisdom*, *Rhadopis of Nubia*, and *Thebes at War*, published in 1939, 1943, and 1944 respectively, have only recently appeared in English, along with a book of short stories set in ancient times, *Voices from the Other World*. His 1985 novella, *Akhenaten, Dweller in Truth*, about the pharaoh who suppressed worship of all deities but the sun god Aton, also came out in English less than a decade ago. These are only a few examples of the complexity of his output in the past seventy years or more.

But not only is Mahfouz brilliant at presenting the living, he is likewise uncanny at conjuring the dead.

For example, Mahfouz's 1945 story, "A Voice from the Other World" is told from the tomb by Taw-ty, a famous versifier and writer in a Nineteenth Dynasty court, who dies of a sudden illness at age twenty-six. Taw-ty watches as his family and friends mourn, bury, and ultimately forget him, while he himself discovers that one should embrace death, not avoid it. Consider his poetic description of his passing from this existence to the next, when the "Messenger of the Hereafter" comes to collect him:

And I saw the holy aura of life surrender to his will, and depart from my feet and my calves and my thighs and my belly and my chest, and the blood within them freeze and the limbs stiffen and the heart stop, until a deep sigh escaped my gaping mouth. My corpse became quiet as I sank into eternity, and the Messenger took his leave just as he came to me, without anyone's noticing. A peculiar feeling pervaded me that I had left life behind, that I had ceased to dwell among the people of the world.[2]

Despite a gap of thirty-four years between them, there is much in common between "A Voice from the Other World" and the title story here, "The Seventh Heaven," published as "al-Sama' al-sabi'a" in the 1979 collection *al-Hubb fawq hadabat al-haram* (*Love on the Pyramids Plateau*). Mahfouz says the idea for "The Seventh Heaven" came while reading a book on encounters with spirits of the departed by Raouf Sadiq Ubayd, former deputy chairman of the College of Law at Cairo's Ayn Shams University. Ubayd's work, *al-Insan ruh la jasad* (*The Human Is a Spirit, not a Body,* 1966),[3] among much else about ghostly phenomena, contains previously unknown poetry allegedly recited in posthumous composition by the spirit of Egypt's "Prince of Poets," Ahmad Shawqi (1868–1932).[4]

"The Seventh Heaven" begins with the almost cinematically described murder of a twentieth-century man, one Raouf Abd-Rabbuh (literally, the "Kind Servant of his Lord"—and not coincidentally including the same first name as the author whose book inspired the story; Mahfouz's characters are rarely, if ever, named at random). Raouf comes to incorporeal consciousness in the afterlife following his death at the hands of a friend with whom he is walking home at the end of a night out. Raouf watches dispassionately as his bloodied body is buried by his killer, Anous (derived from "bachelor, man unable to marry") Qadri ("compelled by fate, fateful")—just as Taw-ty observes his own death and embalming in "A Voice from the Other World"; and in another story in the present collection, "Beyond the Clouds" ("Fawq al-sahab," 1989), a likewise disembodied spirit watches his own family in the throes of grief around his corpse at the moment of his death. Raouf's soul is then received and counseled by a long-expired ancient Egyptian, "Abu, formerly High-Priest at Hundred-Gated Thebes." Abu takes Raouf on a journey through what turns out to be but the first, or lowest, level of the seven heavens. These, of course, are undoubtedly based upon the "seven heavens, one upon another arrayed" *(saba'a samawatin tibaqan)*[5] described in the Qur'an—a concept that long predates Islam in the Near East. In Islamic cosmology, the first heaven is that just above the earth, at the level of the astral bodies, planets, and clouds, which sends rain to grow greenery below. The seventh heaven is where God sits on His throne, in *firdaws* (Paradise), above or near the sacred lote tree, the immortal Tree of Life. The travel distance in time between each heaven and the next in Islamic tradition (not in the Qur'an) is 500 years—for a total journey far short of the "hundreds of thousands of enlightened years" cited in "The Seventh Heaven."[6] Yet humans are not physically reborn after death in the Qur'an (though the dead are to rise on the Day of Judgment). Nor do they return to earth as spiritual guides to the living, as they do in Mahfouz's story, let alone use such invisible influence to drive someone to suicide, as happens in one instance here.

Nor does this story's portrayal of the Other World bear much resemblance to the way the ancient Egyptians conceived it. For them, one either attained an afterlife by surviving the ritual weighing of the heart against the feather of Maat, goddess of order and justice, in the Osiris Court, or died forever as the sin-heavy organ was tossed to the crocodile-headed monster Ammit instead. And, while the number seven was considered fortuitous even in pharaonic times,[7] eternity was essentially in the underworld, not in the heavens. Yet according to the tale of Setna and his son Si-Osiris (dating roughly to the first century A.D.), the boy and man pass through seven halls symbolizing the land of the Dead. In the seventh hall— the place of judgment—sat Osiris, ruler of the nether regions, with his divine entourage.[8] But whatever the similarities and differences between his own post-mortem cartography and those of Islam and the ancient religion, Mahfouz's eschatology is even more unconventional in that he does not depict drastic torments for the truly wicked, but something far subtler than hellfire, or even simple non-existence (which the ancient Egyptians feared most). In "The Seventh Heaven," the twentieth century's two greatest villains, Adolf Hitler and Joseph Stalin, receive nothing more as chastisement than to be reborn in crude conditions on earth, while their quest for Paradise is merely delayed. The banality of evil is matched by the seeming triviality of punishment.

At times, Mahfouz's judgments in the story, "The Seventh Heaven," may strike some as counterintuitive. The chief lackey to Hitler's reincarnation as Boss Qadri the Butcher is none other than Lord Arthur James Balfour (1848–1930), whose November 1917 promise on behalf of the British government to provide a homeland for the Jewish people in Palestine led to the creation of modern Israel. Yet, as viewed from within the Arab political scene since World War II, Mahfouz—who has denounced the Nazis since their heyday, and who has told this writer that "I really miss" the Jews of Egypt[9] (all but a handful of whom left in the 1950s and '60s)—actually reverses here the popular order of villainy in his neighborhood. Throughout the Middle East, Balfour—whose declaration led to the displacement of hundreds of thousands of Palestinians in 1948 and later (as well as the establishment of a haven for Jews persecuted throughout the world)—is widely seen as sinister. Yet Hitler—who millions of Arabs believed would "liberate" them from either British or French colonial rule—has unfortunately been seen as a hero by many in the region. Moreover, in "The Seventh Heaven," Mahfouz makes a sort of benevolent secular prophet out of Vladimir Ilyich Lenin (1870–1924), the ruthless founder of Soviet Communism and instigator of an enormous, and merciless, civil war throughout the Russian empire. He uses a common comparison between the allegedly just and saintly figure of Lenin and the malignant menace of his successor, Stalin. This view was and probably still is popular among many who consider themselves socialist—and Mahfouz still holds it today.[10]

British philosopher Lord Bertrand Russell (1872–1970), who visited Moscow in 1920 to conduct research as a socialist on the new Bolshevist system established in formerly Czarist Russia, draws a different parallel entirely—between Lenin and the nineteenth-century Liberal statesman William Gladstone (1809–1898). In *Unpopular Essays* (1950), Russell recalls:

> *Of the two, I would say that Gladstone was the more unforgettable as a personality. . . . When I met Lenin, I had much less impression of a great man than I had expected; my most vivid impressions were of bigotry and Mongolian cruelty. When I put a question to him about socialism in agriculture, he explained with glee how he had incited the poorer peasants against the richer ones, "and they soon hanged them from the nearest tree—ha! ha! ha!" His guffaw at the thought of those massacred made my blood run cold.*[11]

Whatever one's own views, Mahfouz dexterously deploys the series of afterworld scenes in "The Seventh Heaven" to convey, in extremely brief, deft strokes, his feelings about many of his country's—as well as the world's—most influential figures. In the course of following the poetically interchangeable personae of the story's initial hero (Raouf Abd-Rabbuh) and villain (Anous Qadri) as they each return to earth "condemned" to live once again, Mahfouz has more and more fun with the destinies of the exalted dead. They include a number of Egypt's rulers (such as the "first to bring the news that God is one," Akhenaten (r. *ca.* 1372–1355 B.C.), who are each assigned as earthly guides to prominent national personalities living at the time the story was written—some of whom are still with us today. There is even an incongruous parallel drawn between Mahatma Gandhi and the early Muslim general Khalid bin Walid (d. 642), who defeated the Byzantines at Yarmouk in 636, clearing the way for the stupendous expansion of Islam in the decades that followed.

Raouf's persistent queries disclose the individual verdicts on many major actors. These include a leader of at least two uprisings in Cairo against Napoleon, Umar Makram (1755–1822), dispatched to guide the (still active) newspaper columnist, memoirist, and travel writer Anis Mansur (b. 1924). Another patriotic icon, Ahmad Urabi, leader of the 1882 military revolt that prompted prolonged British control of Egypt, is sent to guide Lewis Awad (1914–1990), the prominent poet, novelist, and critic. Mustafa Kamil (1874–1908), a founder of the National Party, serves Fathi Radwan (1911–1988), an activist in the fascist-inspired Young Egypt movement who later served under Nasser as a minister of information and diplomat. Muhammad Farid (1868–1919), Kamil's successor at the National Party's helm, is assigned to the founder of modern Egypt's greatest construction firm, Osman Ahmed Osman (1917–1999). Only one of the persons that Raouf asks about, Sa'd Zaghlul—Mahfouz's lifelong idol for his role in the early nationalist movement in Egypt—is sent upward to the Second Heaven without having first to do penance as a guide on earth, "because of his triumph over his own human weakness!"

But Zaghlul's successor, Mustafa al-Nahhas—presumably because he was tainted by numerous scandals during his time as Wafd Party leader after Zaghlul, and because he was made prime minister with the aid of British tanks in February 1942—gets off less lightly. First he is sent back down to guide Anwar al-Sadat (still alive at the time this story appeared). But after Sadat's successful military assault on the supposedly impregnable Bar-Lev Line in Israeli-occupied Sinai on October 6, 1973, al-Nahhas is finally allowed to join Zaghlul in the Second Heaven. This neatly permits Mahfouz to unabashedly praise Sadat, the self-styled "Hero of War and Peace," while exonerating the most popular historical figures in his own favorite political party (the Wafd), Zaghlul and al-Nahhas. The censors (and Sadat himself) no doubt took note.

One of the most telling historical cameos is that of U.S. President Woodrow Wilson (1856–1924), who was reviled in Egypt for not pressing one of the basic principles enshrined in his famous Fourteen Points—the self-determination of peoples—upon the British and French empires in the Paris Peace Conference organized by the Allies after World War I. Strangely, in "The Seventh Heaven," Wilson—who did succeed in founding the League of Nations, yet was unable to get the U.S. Congress to approve America's membership in it—is chosen as the spiritual guide for Tawfiq al-Hakim (1898–1987), Mahfouz's own acknowledged mentor and author of Egypt's first nationalist novel, Return of the Spirit (*'Awdat al-ruh*, 1933).

Raouf Abd-Rabbuh asks Abu about Sadat's former patron and immediate predecessor, Gamal Abd al-Nasser.

Abu tells him, "He is now guiding al-Qaddafi." In other words, Mahfouz is mocking Nasser by making him serve the mercurial young colonel who seized power in Libya one year before the Egyptian dictator-colonel's own death in 1970. After all, Mahfouz seems to remind us, al-Qaddafi's idol is Nasser himself; at least in part, we can probably thank Nasser's guidance for the survival of the erratic leader in Tripoli through his shaky early days in power.

Raouf's greatest shock comes when Abu reveals to him that his mother is none other than Rayya, who, with her sister, Sakina, and their respective husbands, had murdered at least thirty women in Alexandria for their jewelry and other valuables by luring them to their homes. Mahfouz wrote the scenario for a renowned 1953 film, *Rayya wa Sakina* (directed by the legendary Salah Abu Seif) about the frightening pair of nefarious forty-somethings and their capture in 1921.[12]

Four years after "The Seventh Heaven" appeared, Mahfouz published a powerful, if peculiar, novel-in-dialogue, *Amam al-'arsh* (*Before the Throne*, 1983). In *Amam al-'arsh*, Mahfouz hauls three score of Egypt's former rulers, from Mina (the possibly apocryphal unifier of ancient Egypt in the First Dynasty), to Anwar al-Sadat, before the Osiris Court for judgment of their performance in power. Asked if "The Seventh Heaven" may have led in any way to his writing *Amam al-'arsh*, Mahfouz would only say, "Not necessarily."[13] Yet the Egyptian leaders who star in the foggy firmament of this "long short story," as the author describes it,[14] had their first taste of Mahfouzian justice in its pages, under the guidance of a priest—however deracinated—from ancient Thebes.

Mahfouz's lifelong obsession with departed spirits also marks his most recent work. *The Dreams* (*Ahlam fatrat al-naqaha*), published in English by the American University in Cairo Press in 2004, is a series of extremely brief vignettes, each said to be based on an actual dream. Like most people's nocturnal visions, Mahfouz's are frequently inhabited by persons long deceased—though most often they are definitely visiting from the land of the Dead, and not simply seen as they were when alive. An excellent example is his old Arabic teacher, Shaykh Muharram, who telephones the dreamer sixty years after his own passing to confess he has learned that many of the lessons he taught him had turned out to be wrong. As a result, the shaykh has come back to give him the corrections. "Having said this," Mahfouz writes, "he laid a folder on the table, and left."[15]

And in the thirteen stories presented here, the same oneiric and unworldly forces are at work in the writer's mind. For example, both "A Man of Awesome Power" ("al-Rajul al-qawi," 1996), and "Forgetfulness" ("al-Nisyan," 1984) feature recurring portentous dreams. Another piece, "The Vapor of Darkness" ("Dukhan al-zalam," 1996) may itself be merely a nightmare—or a frightening memory. In "The Garden Passage" ("Mamarr al-Bustan," 1984), whose name is drawn from an alley in a part of downtown Cairo famed for its secluded bars and artists' cafés, vaguely celestial symbolism mixed with

Sufism, a hint of prostitution, and the uncertain elapse of great spans of time all invoke a feeling of mystic hope and dread combined. "The Rose Garden" ("Hadiqat al-ward," 1999) explores the conflict between the age-old Egyptian reverence for the dead and their tombs as houses for eternal life, and the modern needs of the living in mega-crowded Cairo.

Mahfouz published this story, set in one of Cairo's surviving medieval *hara*s (alleys, quarters), on January 16, 1994, in the women's magazine *Nisf al-dunya* (*Half the World*), where he has debuted nearly all his new fiction since its first issue in February 1990. Nine months later, on October 14, 1994, the then eighty-two-year-old Mahfouz (born December 1911) would be stabbed in the neck, almost fatally, by a religious fanatic in an eerie echo of the fate of this story's unfortunate victim, Hamza Qandil. The attack damaged the nerve that controls his right arm and hand, rendering him able to write little more than his name for over four years. Though by early 1999 he had partially regained his ability to handle a pen, he has lately been forced to dictate new work.

Like Qandil (whose last name means "lamp"), Mahfouz displays more learning than his peers, and his ideas have sometimes put him at odds with local traditions. And he almost paid the same price, exacted in the same way, for roughly the same reasons as his fictional bearer of light. And yet the message of this story, which later appeared in his 1999 collection *Sada al-nisyan* (*The Echo of Forget-fulness*), is somehow ambiguous.

Meanwhile, Qandil's antagonist, Bayumi Zalat, may

have been based on a real local thug of the same name
that the young Mahfouz likely knew in the Darrasa district near his birthplace in the old Islamic quarter of
Gamaliya—and whose grandson I encountered as he
worked parking cars in the neighborhood. Curiously,
Mahfouz's own family's tombs and many others in the
Bab al-Nasr cemetery, likewise close to Gamaliya, were
moved by government decree in an urban renewal scheme
in the 1970s.[16] When asked if "The Rose Garden" had
been inspired by this event, he denied it vehemently.
"No!" he said. "It is a symbolic story—simply!"

Meanwhile, the figure of Death itself materializes not
only in "The Rose Garden" but also in the "The Reception Hall" ("al-Bahw," 1996), in "The Vapor of Darkness"
("Dukhan al-zalam," 1996), and in "Room No. 12" ("al-
Hujra raqm 12," 1973)—in the latter, once as the con-
tractor Yusuf Qabil ("Qabil" is the Qur'anic name for
Cain, the first murderer), and as Blind Sayyid the Corpse
Washer.[17] "The Reception Hall" also highlights Mahfouz's
abiding passion for Sufi imagery, with its moth fluttering
raptly toward the flame, a metaphor favored by the great
Muslim martyr Mansur al-Hallaj, crucified for heresy in
922.[18] Queried jokingly if he had "been inspired by" al-
Hallaj, or had resorted to "literary theft," he chuckled.
"Consider it theft," he quipped.[19]

Another spectral figure who appears more than once in
these stories does so openly in "The Only Man" ("al-
Rajul al-wahid," 1996). But he might also be found more
covertly in "The Disturbing Occurrences" ("al-Hawadith
al-muthira," 1979) as the preternaturally clever character

with a split demonic/angelic personality, and the devilish ability to turn the words of his accusers against them with ease. A further possible clue: he possesses the one trait that in Mahfouz's fictional universe always indicates either a grave moral defect or raving depravity—blond hair. A different kind of deviltry infests "The Haunted Wood" ("al-Ghaba al-maskuna," 1989), an allegory about the literal demonization of dissent in an authoritarian society— amid an ambiguous setting that seems both part of this dimension, and what the narrator calls "the life of the wood." The closing piece, "A Warning from Afar" ("Nadhir min ba'id," 1999) is a kind of prophecy, or a terrorist videotape from the beyond, threatening that the forces of religious fanaticism will sweep in someday to clean out the corruption of this world if we don't watch out. Ironic from a person who was nearly killed by a similar extremism a few years before this story was published— but, as in "The Rose Garden," such nagging nuance is another of Mahfouz's many specialties.

All the stories in this collection of Mahfouz's little-known fiction exploring questions of death, the afterlife, and the disturbingly metaphysical embody what German theologian Rudolf Otto in *The Idea of the Holy* (*Das Heilige*, 1917; English, 1923) called "the numinous." This, as S. L. Varnado says in *Haunted Presence*, his 1987 book reviving Otto's work, "can be summed up as an affective state in which the precipient—through feelings of awe, mystery and fascination—becomes aware of an objective spiritual presence."[20]

The expression "awe, mystery and fascination" derives from Otto's Latin phrase, *mysterium tremendum et fasci-*

nans.[21] That "affective state" is not only invoked by Mahfouz's works dealing with the dead, but by his writings as a whole. Indeed, even by his very being, which exerts awe, mystery, and fascination upon all who know him—whether through his books alone, or in the perishable flesh as well.

———

As translator, I wish to thank Roger Allen, Hazem Azmy, Eric Banks, Brooke Comer, Shirley Johnston, Mary A. Kelly, Ben Metcalf, Abdel Aziz Nossier, Michael Ray, Everett Rowson, Tawfik Saleh, Matthew Stadler, Peter Theroux, Husayn Ukasha, Patrick Werr, and David Wilmsen for their helpful comments on the present work, and Abdalla F. Hassan and R. Neil Hewison for their very fine and proficient editing. And, as always, above all I am grateful to the author, not only for his thoughtful answers about these stories—but for everything.

This translation is dedicated to my sister, Carole Anne Huft, and her husband, David.

NOTES:

1. The lines from "If Ever You Go to Dublin Town" by Patrick Kavanagh are reprinted from *Collected Poems*, edited by Antoinette Quinn (Allen Lane, 2004), by kind permission of the Trustees of the Estate of the late Katherine B. Kavanagh, through the Jonathan Williams Literary Agency.

2. Naguib Mahfouz, *Voices from the Other World: Ancient Egyptian Tales*, translated by Raymond Stock (Cairo and

New York: The American University in Cairo Press, 2002), p. 63.

3. Ra'uf Sadiq 'Ubayd, *al-Insan ruh la jasad*, 2 vols. (Cairo: Dar al-Fikr al-'Arabi, 1966). "Shawqi's" ghostly poetry in Vol. 1, pp. 525–802, and in Vol. 2, pp. 3–16. Other editions of this book also exist.

4. Interview with Naguib Mahfouz, Maadi, February 13, 2002.

5. Qur'an, Surat al-Mulk, 67:3.

6. Jane Dammen MacAuliffe, General Editor, *Encyclopaedia of the Qur'an*, Vol. II (Leiden and Boston: Brill, 2002), pp. 410–13.

7. See Richard B. Parkinson, *The Tale of Sinuhe and Other Ancient Egyptian Poems* (Oxford University Press, 1997), p. 121 *n.*

8. See William Kelly Simpson, ed., *The Literature of Ancient Egypt: An Anthology of Stories, Instructions, Stelae, Autobiographies, and Poetry.* (Cairo: The American University in Cairo Press, 2003), pp. 470–89.

9. Interview with Naguib Mahfouz, Maadi, March 1998.

10. Interview with Naguib Mahfouz, Garden City, October 9, 2005.

11. Bertrand Russell, *Unpopular Essays* (New York: Simon and Schuster, 1950), pp. 170–71. Russell also dug at Gladstone, who, though generally anti-imperialist, sent British troops to put down an uprising in Egypt, where they remained for more than seventy years. On p. 169, he writes, "Invariably he [Gladstone] earnestly consulted his conscience, and invariably his conscience earnestly gave him the convenient answer." Opposition to the British occupation, which ended in 1956, has been a major theme in Mahfouz's works.

12. For Rayya's and Sakina's atrocities and their commemoration in a museum, see Rasha Sadeq, "The Other Citadel," *Al-Ahram Weekly*, February 20–26, 2003. For more on the film, see Samir Farid, *Najib Mahfuz wa-l-sinima* (Cairo: al-Hay'a al-'Amma li-Qusur al-Thaqafa, 1990), p. 18, and Hashim al-Nahhas, *Najib Mahfuz 'ala al-shasha, 1945–1988* (al-Hay'a al-Misriya al-'Amma li-l-Kitab, 1990), pp. 15–27, 243. Also, Hashim al-Nahhas, *Najib Mahfuz wa-l-sinima al-misriya* (Cairo: al-Majlis al-A'la li-l-Thaqafa, 1997), pp. 14, 77–78.

13. Interview with Naguib Mahfouz, Maadi, February 13, 2002. Ditto for quote "long short story"—which, uncharacteristically, Mahfouz offered in English.

14. See also Menahem Milson, *Najib Mahfuz, the Novelist-Philosopher of Cairo* (New York and Jerusalem: St. Martin's Press and The Magnes Press, 1998), pp. 142–43.

15. Naguib Mahfouz, *The Dreams*, translated by Raymond Stock (Cairo and New York: The American University in Cairo Press, 2004), p. 10.

16. Interview with Naguib Mahfouz, *al-Ahram* office, September 1994.

17. In 2005, a half-hour feature (very loosely) based on this story was produced by the Egyptian TV and Radio Union, Nile Thematic TV Channels, entitled *al-Ghurfa raqm 12* (*Room No. 12*), directed by Izz al-Din Sa'id, starring Lutfi Labib, Sahar Rami, Sa'id Abd al-Karim, Ahmad Siyyam, Hasan al-Adl, Kamal Disuqi, with scenario and dialogue by Izz al-Din Sa'id and Makkawi Sa'id.

18. For more on al-Hallaj and the moth, see Joseph Campbell, *The Masks of God: Occidental Mythology* (New York: Penguin Arkana, 1964), p. 447. Also, Roger Allen, *The Arabic*

Literary Heritage (Cambridge University Press, 1998), pp. 64, 192–93, 195, 250, 263, 265, and 347.

19. Interview with Naguib Mahfouz, Garden City, October 9, 2005. The addition of "literary theft" to my question was done by Mohamed el-Kafrawi, a civil engineer and friend of Mahfouz who was sitting as usual by his side.

20. S. L. Varnado, *Haunted Presence: The Numinous in Gothic Fiction* (Tuscaloosa and London: University of Alabama Press, 1987), p. 15.

21. Ibid., p. 10: as Varnado notes, more literally, "a frightening but fascinating mystery."

The Seventh Heaven

The Seventh Heaven

———

A huge cloud surges over all existence, plunging through space. Everything pulses with a strange cosmic presence. Nothing like it has ever been, breaking living beings down into their basic elements, menacing all with destruction— or perhaps a new creation. Despite all this, he is still conscious of what is happening, seeming to live out the last moments of awareness. Seized by sensations that transcend imagination, he is witnessing things that none have seen before. Yet he is still himself—Raouf Abd-Rabbuh— without any fears, without evil whisperings within, and without any cares. He halts in the desert outside the ancient portal, floating in the dark, feeling as though he weighs nothing. He and his friend Anous Qadri are returning from their evening out. *Where are you, Anous?*

He heard not a sound, nor could he feel the touch of the ground. Then he had a bizarre sensation of levitation as he penetrated deeply into the churning, overspreading masses above. When he called out to his friend, no sound issued from him. He was present—and yet was not there at all. He was confused, yet not frightened, though his heart expected a direct reply from close by. The cloud thinned and began to vanish. The pulsing stopped completely. Then the darkness of night glittered with the luminous rays of stars. *Finally I can see now, Anous! But what are you doing?* The people are digging up the earth furiously, and with purpose. Then there is a young man sprawled on his back, blood pouring from his head. Raouf can see with a clarity greater than that granted by the starlight. How amazing! That's Raouf Abd-Rabbuh himself! Yet he is me—and none other than me!

He was cut off from him completely as he watched from very near. No, it's not a double nor his twin. That's definitely his body. And those are his shoes. Anous urges the men on in their work. He does not see him at all. Evidently, he thinks that the body laid out there represents all there is of his friend Raouf Abd-Rabbuh, the creature that observes him, unable to do anything. He sensed that he was not whole like the corpse on the ground. Had he become two beings? Or had he departed from the living? Had he been murdered and suffered death? Did you kill me, Anous? Did we not spend an enjoyable night out together? What did you feel when you killed me? How could you so disdain my friendship that you would try to claim Rashida for yourself? Didn't she tell me that she considered herself to be your sister from now on?

Ah—the men have carried my body to the hole, and are tossing it inside. Now they're shoveling dirt over it and smoothing the spot afterward, restoring the ground to its natural shape. Thus Raouf Abd-Rabbuh vanishes, as though he never was. And yet, Anous, I still exist. You have cleverly buried the evidence of your hardened crime—all trace of it is gone. Yet why are you scowling so? What is that sardonic look in your eyes? I freely confess—even though you cannot hear me—that I still love her. Did you think that our relationship was now over? Even death is too weak to destroy such a passion. Rashida is mine, not yours. Yet you are rash and were raised amidst evil. You grew up in the sphere of your father, Boss Qadri the Butcher—monopolist of the meat trade, plunderer of the poor and the dispossessed, a gross greaser of palms. Let me tell you that what you aspire to is not yours—your felony is to try to gain it by force. What will you do now? You, who wouldn't even go to the café without me, nor study without me, nor come and go to the university without me? We were the two best friends in our quarter, despite the infinite differences between us in money, status, and power. You may forget me, but I will not forget you. You should know that I have no longing for vengeance, or to hurt you in any way. All such weaknesses were buried with my body in that hole in the ground. Even the torture that your father's oppression inflicts on our alley provokes neither rage nor wrath nor rebellion within me. Rather, it is a common occurrence that the power of love rejects, creating instead a lofty desire free of any stain. I mourn for you, Anous. I never conceived you in this ugly image before. You are a walking skeleton, a bat-infested ruin. Murdered blood splotches your face and your brow. Your eyes give off sparks, while a serpent hangs from each of your ears. Your father's men file behind you on donkeys' hooves, with heads like crows, bound in manacles bolted with thorns. How it saddens me to have been the cause for which you sullied your pages. I am overwhelmed with grief because of it—while my sense of happiness shrinks to nothing.

2

In the midst of a sigh, Raouf found himself in a new city—brilliantly illuminated, but without a sun. The sky was a cupola of white clouds, the ground rich with greenery, with endless orchards of flowering fruit trees. Stretching into the distance were rows of white roses. Throngs of people met and broke up with the fleetness of birds. In an empty spot, he felt the loneliness of the first-time arrival. At that moment, there arose before him a man enshrouded in a white mist.

"Welcome, Raouf," the man said, smiling, "to the First Heaven."

"Is this Paradise?" Raouf asked, shouting with joy.

"I said, 'the First Heaven,' not 'Paradise,'" the stranger admonished.

"Then where is Paradise?"

"Between it and you, the path is very, very long," the man answered. "The fortunate person will spend hundreds of thousands of enlightened years traversing it!"

A sound like a groan escaped Raouf. "Permit me first

to introduce myself," said the man. "I am your interlocutor, Abu, formerly High Priest at Hundred-Gated Thebes."

"I'm honored to meet you, Your Reverence. What a happy coincidence that I'm Egyptian myself!"

"That is of no importance," replied Abu. "I lost all nationality thousands of years ago. Now I am the defense counsel appointed by the courts for the new arrivals."

"But there can be no charge against me—I'm a victim. . . ."

"Patience," Abu said, cutting him off. "Let me tell you about your new surroundings. This heaven receives the new arrivals. They are tried in court, where I serve as their advocate. The verdicts are either for acquittal or for condemnation. In case of acquittal, the defendant spends one year here spiritually preparing for his ascent to the Second Heaven."

Raouf interrupted him, "But what then does 'condemnation' mean?"

"That the condemned must be reborn on earth to practice living once again; perhaps they would be more successful the next time," said Abu. "As for verdicts that fall between acquittal and condemnation, in such cases the accused is usually put to work as a guide to one or more souls on earth. Depending on their luck, they may ascend to the Second Heaven, or the length of their probationary period might be extended, et cetera."

"At any rate, I'm definitely innocent," Raouf blurted confidently. "I lived a good life and died a martyr."

"Do not be so hasty," Abu counseled him. "Let us open the discussion of your case. Identify yourself, please."

"Raouf Abd-Rabbuh, eighteen years of age, a university

student of history. My father died, leaving my mother a widow who lives on a charitable trust from the Ministry of Religious Endowments."

"Why are you so satisfied with yourself, Raouf?" queried Abu.

"Well, despite my intense poverty, I'm a hard-working student who loves knowledge, for which my thirst is never quenched."

"That is beautiful, as a matter of principle," remarked Abu, "yet you received most of your information from others, rather than through your own thinking."

"Thought is enriched through age and experience," said Raouf. "And regardless, would that count as a charge against me?"

"Here a person is held accountable for everything," rejoined Abu. "I observe that you were dazzled by new ideas."

"The new has its own enchantment, Your Reverence Abu," said Raouf.

"First of all, do not call me, 'Your Reverence,'" Abu rebuked him. "Second, we do not judge a thought itself even when it is false. Rather, we denounce submission to any idea, even if it is true."

"Such a cruel trial! Justice on earth is far more merciful."

"We will come to justice," Abu reassured him. "How did you find your alley?"

"Horrible," spat Raouf. "Most of the people there are poor beggars. They are controlled by a man who monopolizes all the food—and who has bought the loyalty of the shaykh of the *hara*. He kills, steals, and lives securely above the law."

"That is an accurate description," Abu said. "What was your position toward all this?"

"Rejection, rebellion, and a genuine desire to change everything."

"Thank you. What did you do to achieve that?"

"It wasn't in my power to do anything!"

"Do you want to rise to the Second Heaven?"

"Why shouldn't I rise?" Raouf shot back. "My heart and mind both rejected what was happening."

"And your tongue?"

"Just one rebellious word would get it cut out."

"Yet even speech by itself would not satisfy our sacred tribunal," warned Abu.

"What kind of proceeding is this!" Raouf asked, his frustration growing. "What was I, after all, but a single individual?"

"Our alley here is full of unfortunates," rebutted Abu.

"My first duty was to acquire knowledge!"

"There is no dividing one's trust—and no excuse for evading it."

"Wouldn't one expect that would lead to violence?"

"Virtues do not interest us," said Abu dismissively. "What concerns us is truth."

"Doesn't it help my case that I was murdered over love?"

"Even that has an aspect which is not in your favor," said Abu.

Astonished, Raouf asked, "And what aspect is that?"

"That you put your faith in Anous Qadri—when he is the very image of his tyrannical father."

"I never dreamed I was so guilty."

"Though you have some mitigating circumstances, my brief in defending you will not be easy," worried Abu.

"Ridiculous to think anyone has ever succeeded in being declared innocent in this court."

"Indeed, only a rare few discharge their full obligation to the world."

"Give me some examples," Raouf challenged Abu.

"Khalid bin Walid, and Gandhi."

"Those are two totally contradictory cases!"

"The tribunal has another view," said Abu. "The obligation itself is what matters."

"There's no hope for me now."

"Do not despair—nor should you underestimate my long experience," said Abu soothingly. "I will do the impossible to save you from condemnation."

"But what could you say on my behalf?"

"I will say that you had a blameless beginning, under the most arduous conditions, and that much good was expected of you if you had only lived long enough. And that you were a loving, devoted, faithful son to your mother."

"The best I can hope for, then, is to be made someone's spiritual guardian?" Raouf fretted.

"This is a chance for you to recapture what had eluded you," Abu consoled him. "In our world here, the human being only ascends according to his success on earth."

"Then, Mighty Advocate, why don't you send down a guide for Boss Qadri the Butcher?"

"There is no one who does not have their own guide."

"How then," Raouf asked in confusion, "can evil continue?"

"Do not forget that the human being has free will," replied Abu. "In the end, everything depends upon the influence of the guide and the freedom of the individual."

"Wouldn't it be in the cause of good to eliminate this freedom?"

"The Will has determined that only the free may gain admission to the heavens."

"How could He not admit into heaven the pure saint of our alley, Shaykh Ashur?" Raouf remonstrated. "He doesn't practice free will, for all he does or says is filled with righteous inspiration."

Abu smiled. "What is he but a creation of Qadri the Butcher? He interprets dreams in Qadri's interests, relaying to him the private confidences from inside the houses that welcome his blessings!"

Raouf lapsed into defeated silence. He absented himself for a moment amid the ripe greenery adorned with rows of blooming roses, surrendering to the place's sweetness and grace. Then he said, sighing, "How tragic for a person to be forced to abandon this garden!"

"Be warned—it is sinful to wish to evade your duty!" Abu scolded.

"When shall I appear before the court?" Raouf asked.

"The trial is finished," announced Abu.

Raouf stared at him in stupefaction.

"The examination has been completed," said Abu calmly. "The defense was raised during the discourse between you and me. The verdict has come down: you are to be commissioned as a spiritual guide. Congratulations!"

3

The court determined to hold Raouf Abd-Rabbuh in the First Heaven for a short time in order to cleanse him of any stains, in preparation for his mission. Abu stayed at his side till he had finished his training and acclimation, receiving returning guides at the same time.

"I'd like to see Adolf Hitler," said Raouf. "Will he be coming now?"

"He was condemned, and has since been reborn in your very own alley. You saw him regularly."

"Hitler?"

"He is Boss Qadri the Butcher."

Dumbfounded, Raouf became quiet, then asked, "So who would the shaykh of the *hara*, Shakir al-Durzi, be?"

"Lord Balfour."

"And Shaykh Ashur, the false friend of God?"

"He is Khunfus, betrayor of Urabi's Revolution."

"I don't see them changing or learning from their repeated experience."

"That is not always the case. Do you know who your mother was?"

"Abu, she was an angel, surely!"

"She was Rayya, the infamous serial killer; yet look how she has progressed!"

Shaken, Raouf fell silent again. Just then Abu received the first of the incoming arrivals.

The one who just arrived said, "I am trying as hard as I can."

"I am aware of that," Abu answered, "but you must redouble your efforts, for the time has come for you to go up."

"I'm sure I know who that is," Raouf said, when the man had disappeared. "Isn't he Akhenaten?"

"Indeed he is. He is not very fortunate, however, for his probation has stretched on now for thousands of years."

"But he was the first to bring the news that God is one!"

"Verily, but he imposed the One God on the people by coercion, rather than by persuasion and rational argument. Hence, he made it easier for his enemies to later remove God from people's hearts the same way—by force. If it were not for his clear conscience, he would have been condemned."

"Why has his period here been so prolonged?"

"He did not succeed with any of those he was chosen to guide, such as Pharaoh-in-the-time-of-Moses, al-Hakim bi-Amr Allah, and Abbas I."

"Who is his man now?"

"Camille Chamoun."

The next arrival approached; he delivered a written report, uttered some stirring words, then vanished completely. "That was President Wilson!" Raouf exclaimed.

"You are correct."

"I'd assumed he was one of the happy few who'd risen to the Second Heaven."

"You are no doubt referring to his sacred principles," observed Abu. "But you forget that he neglected to use America's power to implement them—and that he recognized the protectorate over Egypt."

"And who's *his* man?"

"The eminent littérateur, Tawfiq al-Hakim."

When the third arrival had gone, Raouf declared, "That was Lenin—no doubt about it."

"Correct again," affirmed Abu.

"I'd have thought he'd be condemned on account of his atheism," Raouf gasped. "What did you say in his defense?"

"I said that in the stream of intellectual prattle, he changed the names—but not the essence—of things. Perishable matter he termed divine, assigning it some of the qualities of God—timelessness, creation, and control over the fate of the universe. He called the prophets scientists, the angels workers, and the devils the bourgeoisie. He also promised a paradise on earth, which exists in time and space. I extolled the power of his belief and his bravery, as well as his service to the laboring classes through sacrifice and self-denial. I added that what really mattered to God Almighty was whether good or bad befell humankind. As for He Himself—His majesty be praised—He has no need of human beings. Not all their faith can increase Him, nor their disbelief diminish Him. Hence, Lenin's sentence was reduced—and he was appointed as a spiritual guide!"

"Who did he get?" Raouf asked breathlessly.

"The well-known writer, Mustafa Mahmud."

"And was Stalin, too, appointed anyone's guide?"

"Certainly not. Stalin was condemned for having murdered millions of workers, rather than teaching and training them for a better life."

"Maybe he's living now in our alley," Raouf pondered.

"No, he is toiling in one of the pit mines of India," said Abu.

After receiving Lenin, Abu was done with his scheduled appointments, so he accompanied Raouf on a tour through the First Heaven. No sooner had the idea occurred to them than they were already on their way, in response to their inner wish, without needing even to use their feet. They soared like birds, intoxicated with an integral ecstasy that sprang from their magical powers to make any desired movement with ease and delight. They sluiced through the silvery air over the land embroidered with green below, the sky overhead illuminated with glowing white clouds. They passed by countless faces of multifarious races and colors, each absorbed in their lofty enterprise: to help the people of earth achieve progress and victory. In so doing, they seek to repent and purify themselves in order to resume their own rise through the levels of spiritual creativity, to be nearer to the Great Truth itself. They labor relentlessly, driven by warm, eternal passions toward perfection, right, and immortality.

"It seems to me," Raouf said, "there is no less suffering here than in its counterpart on earth."

A smiling Abu replied, "They are two sorts of suffering which join into one. The only difference is that here people experience it with a purer heart, a smarter brain, and a clearer goal."

"Please spell that out for me, Abu."

"You on the earth dream of a world containing the virtuous city, founded on individual freedom, social justice, scientific progress, and overwhelming power over the forces of nature. For the sake of all this, you wage war and make peace, and challenge the Opposing Power that—in your own terminology—you call reactionism. That is all fine and beautiful, but it is not the final objective, as you imagine it to be. Rather, it is but the first real step in a long road to spiritual elevation, which seems even to those who dwell in our First Heaven to be without end."

Raouf was immersed in contemplation until Abu asked him, "Of what are you thinking?"

"I'm thinking how much dreadful, daily crime is perpetrated by the Opposing Power."

"That is crime in which the good take part by passively abstaining in the fight for the right," said Abu. "They fear death—and death is what you see here!"

"What a life!" said Raouf.

"It is a battlefield—nothing more, and nothing less."

Raouf thought until the very thinking wore him out, then returned to his previous passion for learning the destinies of people who interested him. "I'd like to know what's become of my country's leaders," he told Abu.

"You could wait until you see them—or ask me now about whomever you like," the ex–High Priest replied.

"What about al-Sayyid Umar Makram?"

"He is the guide to Anis Mansur," said Abu.

"And Ahmad Urabi?" Raouf asked.

"He is working with Lewis Awad."

"And Mustafa Kamil?"

"He is helping Fathi Radwan."

"Muhammad Farid?"

"The mentor to Osman Ahmed Osman," said Abu.

"And what of Sa'd Zaghlul?"

"He has reached the Second Heaven," intoned Abu.

"Because of his personal sacrifices?" said Raouf, expectantly.

"Because of his triumph over his own human weakness!"

"Again, please tell me what you mean."

"You may be aware that he suffered from the sin of ambition before the revolution," said Abu. "Afterward, however, he rose to become an exquisite vision of courage and devotion—and hence merited acquittal."

"And Mustafa al-Nahhas?"

"He was attached to Anwar al-Sadat," noted Abu. "But when October 6 came, and freedom was restored, he, too, rose to the Second Heaven."

"Then what about Gamal Abd al-Nasser?" the slain man asked.

"He is now guiding al-Qaddafi."

———

At the end of the brief training period, Abu told Raouf, "You are now the spiritual guide to your murderer, Anous, Qadri the Butcher's son."

Raouf accepted the order with zealous resolve.

"Rely on your own mind for inspiration—for it has great power if you master its use," instructed Abu. "When necessary, you may even resort to dreams—and may the Lord be with you."

4

Raouf Abd-Rabbuh landed in the alley. He could see and hear clearly, though no one saw or heard him. He moved from place to place like a natural breeze through his beloved quarter, with all its solid and familiar scenes, its people engrossed in the affairs of life. All his memories were unchanged, along with his previous hopes and pains. He enjoyed a clarity of mind like a brilliant light. Scores and scores of laborers, both men and women, toiled away with furtive eyes and brawny forearms. The laughter floated over the curses, like sweet butter spoiled by bitter mold. And there was Boss Qadri the Butcher in his shop. No resemblance between his face and Hitler's, but his body was bloated from sucking people's blood. And here is Lord Balfour—that is, Shakir al-Durzi, the shaykh of our alley, who throws the law under the butcher's feet. And there is the bogus *wali*, Shaykh Ashur, who foretells the future to flatter his lord and master.

My poor alley. May God be with you! How and when shall you burst these binding fetters?

Evidently, his own absence—that of Raouf—had stirred the alley's tongues as well as its hearts. The women gathered round his weeping mother.

"This is the third day since he disappeared," she moaned.

"Umm Raouf, you should tell the police," they urged.

"I've already told 'Uncle' Shakir al-Durzi, shaykh of the *hara*," she said.

The shaykh's voice came to them scornfully, "Do young people today have no shame?"

"My son has never spent a whole night away from his home," she said, still weeping.

And here is Rashida returning from her institute, the beauty of her tawny face marred by melancholy. Her mother said to her, "Take care of yourself—you can't replace your health when it's gone."

Choking back tears, she said, "I know. My heart never lies to me!"

Raouf stared at her with sympathy. *I believe you, Rashida. A loving heart is the most reliable receptor of truth. Yet we will meet again one day. Love is undying, Rashida, not like some people imagine it to be.*

And here is the killer, swaggering home from the university. He holds a book in one hand, while he commits murder with the other! *I am never out of your thoughts, yet you have no idea that I've been appointed your spiritual mentor. Shall you yield to me today, or persist in your error? Everything calls out to reassure you, Anous. Your father casts his shadow over all. The government and all authority are his loyal subjects—you can get any false testimony you need. Yet my image never leaves you. And why not? Did not people say that our friendship was proverbially close? Though trained in criminality, you didn't practice it like your father. In the course of your education, you learned, or at least heard, of beautiful things. By committing this travesty, did you dream you would win Rashida's heart? What was this that you slew and buried in the desert? What you have done has not hurt me more than it has you. I was your eternal companion, as you shall see. Confess, Anous. Admit your crime. Tell the truth and stick with me—and you will have a better part to play in all this.*

Here is my tormented mother, blocking your path.

"Master Anous," she pleaded, "do you have any news of your friend?"

"None at all, by God," he swore.

"He told me as he went out that he was going to see you."

"We met for a few minutes," said Anous, "then he told me he had to do an important errand, and that we would meet tonight at the café."

"But he hasn't come back," the distraught mother said.

"Didn't I visit you asking about him?"

"That's true, my dear boy, but I'm about to lose my mind."

"I'm as upset as you are," declared Anous.

Believe me, Anous. I see the distress in your soul like a blemish on your face. But you are malignant and cruel. You are from the Opposing Power, Anous—don't you see the danger in that? We grumble all the way down the Path of Light—so what do you think about while sliding down the Path of Darkness? I am stuck to you. If you don't taste that roasted chicken, then the fault is yours. If you can't concentrate on the book you're reading, that's your own problem, as well. I will never leave you, nor shall I ever grow tired. You may as well stay up late, for you shall not know sleep before dawn.

When he rose back to the First Heaven, Raouf encountered Abu deep in discussion with Akhenaten.

"Every time I told him to go right, he went left!" the defunct pharaoh fumed.

"You must use your powers as needed," exhorted Abu.

"We lack the ability to use physical force," Akhenaten complained.

"Do you want to go up, or do you not?" exploded Abu. "The trouble is, you are not used to persuading and convincing people of your point of view. You only know how to give orders!"

Abu turned to Raouf. "How are things with you?" he asked.

"I'm off to a good start," the youngster said.

"Wonderful!" said Abu.

"Yet I wonder, doesn't everyone have their own guide?"

"Naturally," said Abu.

"Then why does everyone just give up?"

"How wrong you are," Abu abjured. "You were born in the age of revolutions!"

At that moment, a green bird the size of an apple landed on Abu's shoulder. It brought its rose-colored beak close to Abu's ear. Abu seemed to be listening, when the bird suddenly flew off into space until it was hidden behind a white cloud.

Abu looked meaningfully into Raouf's eyes. "That was the messenger from the Second Heaven," he explained, "bringing word of the acquittal and right to ascend for one called Sha'ban al-Minufi."

"Who's he?" asked Raouf.

"An Egyptian soldier who was martyred at Morea in the age of Muhammad Ali. He was mentor to a hard-currency smuggler named Marwan al-Ahmadi—and finally succeeded in his campaign to drive him to suicide."

Sha'ban al-Minufi approached, wrapped in his vaporous robe. "May you ascend gloriously and with grace to the Second Heaven," Abu told him.

All the spiritual guides flocked toward them in the shape of white doves until the verdant place was packed, Sha'ban al-Minufi's face beaming in their midst. As celestial music sounded, Abu declaimed, "Rise, O rose of our green city, to carry on your sacred struggle."

In a pleasing voice, Sha'ban replied, "Blessings upon whoever renders service to the suffering world."

At this he began to go up with the lightness of an ephemeral fragrance to the strains of the happy anthem of farewell.

5

Anous Qadri, the butcher's son, stood facing the police detective who asked him, "When was the last time you saw Raouf Abd-Rabbuh?"

"The afternoon of the day he disappeared," said Anous. "He came to see me at my house. No sooner had he showed up than he left to do some business. He promised to meet me that evening at the café."

"Did he tell you anything about this business he had to do?"

"No," said Anous.

"Did you ask him about it?" the officer pressed him.

"No, I thought it must be something to do with his family."

"Some people saw the two of you walking together in the alley after he came to you," the detective informed him.

———————

Don't be upset. The best thing is to confess. This is your golden opportunity, if you know what's good for you.

———————

"I walked with him till he left the gate," said Anous.

"You mean he simply disappeared in the desert outside?"

———————

This is doubletalk, Anous—even worse than doubletalk. Only the truth can save you.

———————

"Yes, he did," answered Anous.

"What did you do after that?"

"I went to the coffeehouse to wait for him."

"How long did you stay there?" the detective continued.

"Until midnight, then I went home."

"Can you prove that?"

"Shakir al-Durzi, shaykh of the *hara*, was sitting next to me the whole time," said Anous. "Early the next morning, I went to Raouf's place to ask his mother about him. She told me that he hadn't come back."

"What did you do?"

"I asked all our friends and acquaintances in the alley about him."

"Do you have any personal insight into his prolonged disappearance?" the policeman asked.

"Not at all! It's truly baffling," insisted Anous.

———————

Here you are leaving the station, Anous. You prepare in advance every word you speak. You rue the mention of the gate, and wonder who saw you walking there with me. It's as though you are contemplating more evil. You repeat the details of your conversations to your father. He is strident—the money, the law, and the witnesses are all in his pocket. I counsel you again to confront your crime with courage and to clear your account. But what's this? Does Rashida's image still trace itself in your imagination? This is the very essence of madness. Then you see that the inquiries about you will continue like a flood. The shaykh of the alley has come to the same conclusion. The Unseen warns of unknown surprises. You are thinking of all this, and at the same time you're obsessed with Rashida, you fool!

Reflecting on this, Raouf remarked to Abu, "Fear of death is the greatest curse to afflict humankind."

"Was it not created to prevent them from doing wrong?" Abu replied.

Raouf was silent as Abu added, "You were appointed as a guide, not a philosopher—remember that."

6

You're asking yourself, Anous, why did the detective summon you a second time? Things are not turning out as simply as you thought.

Here is the officer questioning you:

"What do you know about Raouf's private life?"

"Nothing worth mentioning."

"Really?" the detective challenged him. "What about his love for Rashida, the student in the school of fashion design?"

"Every young man has a relationship like that!" Anous said dismissively.

"Do you have one like it?"

"These are personal things that have no place in an investigation."

"Is that what you think?" the officer shot back. "Even when you love the same girl yourself?"

"The issue needs clarification," protested Anous.

"Good!" exclaimed the policeman. "What could that be?"

"I revealed to Raouf once that I wanted to get engaged to Rashida, and he confided in me that the two of them were in love with each other," Anous asserted. "At that I excused myself, and considered the subject closed."

"But love doesn't end with a word," scoffed the detective.

"It was nothing but a fleeting feeling. . . . I don't know what you mean!"

"I'm gathering information, and I'm wondering if your feelings for your friend haven't changed, if only just a little?"

"Absolutely not," answered Anous. "My emotions for Rashida were nothing special—but my friendship with Raouf was the kind that lasts a lifetime."

"You said, *was*—has it ended?"

"I meant," Anous said nervously, "that our friendship is for life."

———

You're wondering, how is the investigation proceeding with Rashida? What has she admitted? Fine. Let me tell you that the inquiry is ongoing. She has told them of your attempt to rip her from your friend's heart. Just as she told them of your father's omnipotence, and her fear for her own and her mother's safety. I guarantee you, things really are now going against you.

———

"You sound as though you've given up on seeing your friend again," the detective taunted, laughing.

"I'm sure he's coming back," sputtered Anous. "That's what my heart tells me."

"A believer's heart is his guide," said the officer. "I, too, want him to come back."

———

You're leaving the police station, even more disturbed than you were the last time. I think you sensed that this clever little gumshoe suspects you completely, and you don't believe your father is able to control everything. Did not Hitler himself suffer final defeat—and even kill himself in the end?

7

The detective has called you back for a third session, Anous. Nerves are starting to fray. Your father stares at Shakir al-Durzi with fury, but what can the shaykh really do? Stop in front of your tormentor, the officer, and listen:

"Anous, we've received an anonymous letter that accuses you of killing your friend, Raouf."

"A contemptible charge," Anous shouted with spurious rage. "Let whoever made it show his face!"

"Be patient," the officer warned him. "We weigh everything accurately here. Didn't you and your friend often spend evenings together outside the gate?"

"Sure," Anous acknowledged.

"Where, then, did you two spend your time in that vast desert?"

"In the Nobles' Coffeehouse on the plateau."

"I've decided to conduct a face-to-face meeting between you, Anous, and the men in the café."

———

Hold on, don't be distressed. You are stubborn—that's the truth. You don't want to respond to my secret whisperings. Be sure that I'm working in your interest, Anous.

———

The meeting took place. The owner of the coffeehouse and his young helper testified that they hadn't seen Anous for more than a month. That he was not entirely convinced showed clearly on the detective's face. He glared at Anous harshly.

"Please get out," the officer told him.

———

You're leaving the station again, a grin of victory on your lips. You have the right to feel that way—for your father has thrown up a defensive line all around you. But will the affair really end there? Your heart is palpitating while you pass your days loitering in front of your victim's house. Anxiety assails you yet again. Who was the unknown person who sent the letter accusing you? And will there be any more like it? You are a killer, Anous, and your conscience doesn't want to awake. Just let me visit you tonight in a dream—for so long as you won't respond to my clandestine appeals, you will find my corpse stretched out next to you on your bed. Ah—here your scream arises, propelled by your nightmare. You awake in terror, your heart heavy with horror. You slither from your bed to moisten your throat with a gulp of water. Yet you find the cadaver with you again as soon as you slip back to sleep. And the dream recurs to you night after night. Your mother urges Shaykh Ashur to examine you. He gives you an amulet to wear over your heart—but my grisly remains will not leave your dreams. Your condition worsens, so you go secretly to see a psychiatrist, with regular visits week after week. He tells you something truly astounding: that you imagine your friend has been murdered—his body represents your own body, due to the emotional bond between you—you are so closely linked that you think that his body is in the place of yours. But why do you picture yourself as the one slain? Your body plays the role of the replacement for another body and another person that, deep down, you'd like to kill. That person is your father. Your father thus is the cause of your dream—all of which reflects an Oedipus complex!

Yet, in reality, you are not courting your mother, nor do you really want to murder your father. Rather, you are in love with Rashida—and you murdered me simply to get me out of the way.

Raouf railed about this clinical error to his spiritual advocate.

"The complaints of incorrect scientific diagnosis are many," commiserated Abu. "Frustration is mistaken for an illness arising from the consumption of chocolate. Depression caused by loss of faith results in treatment of the sympathetic nerves. Constipation due to the political situation prompts a prescription of laxatives—and so on."

"What to do then, Abu?"

"Have you yet reached despair?"

"Absolutely not," insisted Raouf.

"Then put all your strength into your task," urged Abu.

8

The cause of Raouf Abd-Rabbuh's disappearance remained undetected, while the incident itself slowly faded from people's minds. The only ones who still thought of him were his mother and Rashida. Meanwhile, Anous continued to practice his normal way of living absorbed in work and amusing himself. The past pursued him from time to time, both in his waking hours and in sleep, but he tamed and controlled his internal uproar through sedatives, narcotics, and sheer force of will. With the legal side now completely subdued, Anous once again began to fix his thoughts on Rashida—for why else would he have undertaken the most horrific act of his life? He lay in wait to see her every morning as they went to their respective institutes to study. Was her face still set in the pain of remembrance, hasn't she lost hope yet? Does she never think of her future as a young woman who should seek life, happiness, marriage, and children? Doesn't she aspire to have the man who could offer her the most in our whole quarter?

His mad gambit in devotedly pursuing her and his unshakeable desire to totally possess her had only intensified. Once, as she passed the place where he was seated on a tram, he called out to her in greeting—but she ignored him completely.

"We should be helping each other!" he called to her.

She wrinkled her brow in disgust, but he kept talking to her, "We've each lost a dear one that we both shared!"

At this she broke her silence, "He wasn't lost, he was murdered!"

"What?" Anous recoiled.

"Many people believe that," she said.

"But he didn't have a single enemy!"

She glared at him with contempt, and said no more.

———

"She was accusing you of killing him," Anous told himself. "Do you have any doubt about that? You could erase the crime from your record if you rose up to confront your father—but the time for love has already gone."

———

She got off the tram before him. As he followed her movements with longing and resentment, his imagination was seized by uncontrollable visions of lust and violence.

9

"Everyone's talking about that amazing man who summons the dead," Rashida's mother said. "So why don't you give him a try, since it won't even cost you a single millieme!"

Raouf's stricken mother stared at her in confusion, then muttered, "If you'll go with me."

"Why not? I'll get in touch with Rashida's dearly departed father."

"Many respectable people believe in the art of contacting the spirits," interrupted Rashida, who had been following their conversation with interest.

And so, under the strictest secrecy, they made an appointment to try this experiment.

Raouf turned to Abu jubilantly, "This is my chance to expose the culprit!"

"You were assigned as a guide for him—not against him," rebuked Abu.

"Would you let this opportunity slip out of our hands?"

"You are not a police counselor, Raouf," Abu cautioned him. "You are a spiritual advisor. Your goal is to save Anous, not deliver him to the hangman."

"But he's like a hunk of rock. The winds of wisdom simply bounce right off him," Raouf rejoined.

"That is a confession of your own incapacity."

"No, I haven't given up yet," Raouf said excitedly. "But what should I do if they call upon my spirit?"

"You are free," replied Abu. "It would not benefit your freedom to seek guidance from me."

The séance was convened, attended by Raouf's mother, along with Rashida and her own mother. They appealed to Raouf beyond the veil of the Unseen—and he entered the darkened chamber.

"Raouf greets you, mother," he called, in a voice that all present could hear.

"What happened to you, Raouf?" she said, sobbing at the confirmation that her son was dead.

"Don't be sad, mother," he answered without hesitation. "I am happy. Only your sorrow grieves me. My greetings to you too, Rashida. . . ."

With that, he instantly rushed from the room.

10

Raouf's mother, Rashida, and her own mother returned from the séance, asking each other, "Why didn't he reveal the secret of his murder?"

"He was taken in the prime of his youth!" Raouf's mother lamented, drying her tears.

"Don't sadden him with your mourning," implored Rashida.

"Who knows? Maybe he died in an accident," her mother wondered.

"But why didn't he tell us how he died?" Raouf's mother persisted.

"That's his secret, whatever it is!" insisted Rashida.

The séances became Raouf's mother's sole consolation in life; she would go to them accompanied by both

Rashida's mother and Rashida. But in the final days before her exams, Rashida stopped taking part in them.

On one of these nights, as she was at home studying on her own, Anous Qadri burst into the room. He had slunk up the open central stairwell of her building, then forced his way in. Raouf shouted at him to go back where he had come from, and not to take a single step toward her. But Anous attacked Rashida, stifling her voice by jamming his palm over her mouth.

"You're going to run after *me* from now on, you . . . you stubborn bitch!" he snarled.

Then he began to brutally assault her, as she resisted as hard as she could, but to no avail.

"I'm going to take you alive or dead!" he taunted her.

Her hand groped for a pair of scissors on the table. With an insane strength, despite being pinned under his heavy weight, she plunged it into the side of his neck. He pressed upon her with vicious cruelty. Then his vitality ebbed away until he fell motionless upon her body, his warm blood pouring over her face and her torn blouse.

She threw him off of her and he lay sprawled on the tattered carpet. Then she staggered to the window and shrieked at the top of her lungs.

11

The people came running to the apartment, where they found Rashida like a demented murderess spattered with gore. They saw Anous' body and started to scream, while

Rashida curled into herself like a ball, murmuring, "He wanted to rape me. . . ."

If not for the arrival of the detective and the shaykh of the *hara*, then the news might have led Boss Qadri the Butcher to murder her on the spot.

"My son—my only son!" he roared. "I will make the world burn!"

"Everyone out now!" the officer ordered, as his assistants surrounded Rashida.

"I will drink your blood," said Qadri, aiming his storming rage at the girl.

The news soon spread like wildfire through their quarter.

12

Anous stared insensibly down at his body. Raouf came up to him, smiling, as the other looked at him and blurted, "Raouf, what brought you here?"

"The same thing that brought you here," he replied. "Come along with me quickly, far away from this room."

"And leave this behind?" Anous asked, still peering at his corpse.

"That is your old robe. It won't do you any good to wear it now!"

"Have I . . . have I . . . ?" Anous stuttered.

"Yes, you have departed the world, Anous."

He was silent for a while, then he said, referring to Rashida, "But she is innocent."

"I am aware of that," Raouf assured him. "But you can't save her—so come with me."

"I'm sorry for what I did to you," said Anous.

"Regret has no importance."

"I'm glad to see you," answered Anous.

"And I'm glad to see you," responded Raouf.

13

Raouf rapidly began to acquaint Anous with his new environs, then told him, "Here is Abu—your lawyer," when the ancient ex-Egyptian arrived.

"Welcome, Anous, to the First Heaven," said Abu.

"You mean, it was written that I should go to heaven?" Anous asked in shock.

"Be patient. The road is much longer than you conceive," Abu replied with his well-practiced smile.

Abu then began to inform him of the facts he needed to know about his new world, about the system of trials, and the kinds of verdicts to expect in them. He paraded Anous' beastly actions in front of him like ugly ghosts, until the young man's face grimaced and—wobbling with despair—he could endure no more.

Despite this, Abu said, "In any case, it is my mission to defend you."

"Is there a chance you could succeed in that?" Anous pleaded. "Will it lighten the burden of my sins that I was deprived of life at an early age?"

"You lost it at the hand of a girl defending her honor as

you attacked her. Then you left her facing a charge for your murder."

"That's true," admitted Anous. "How I wish I could become her spiritual guide."

"She was successful, as was her spiritual mentor. She has no need of you."

"Does that mean I'm damned?"

"No doubt your father lurks behind your corruption," said Abu. "He is the one who led you astray, who filled you with selfishness, who suggested that you harm people, who whispered in your ear that you should perpetrate crimes as though you owned the whole world."

"You've spoken the truth," Anous said animatedly, seeing his hopes revived.

"Yet, since you have your own mind, heart, and will, you are judged on your own account," said Abu.

"My father's power numbed all my powers completely!"

"Heaven holds you responsible for yourself—and for the world altogether."

"Isn't that responsibility far above the abilities of any human being?"

"But you bear it in exchange for the gift of life itself," reproved Abu.

"But I was born without any say in the matter!"

"Rather, you took this pact upon yourself while you were still in the womb."

"In all honesty, I have no memory of that."

"It is incumbent upon you to remember."

"This is a prosecution, not a defense!"

"We must establish the truth," explained Abu.

"I was not without good qualities—I sought knowledge, and I loved sincerely, as well," said Anous.

"You sought knowledge merely as a means to achieve status, while your love was but a presumptuous urge to possess the girl who belonged to your poverty-stricken friend."

"She never left my mind for one moment. . . ."

"That was nothing but arrogance and desire."

Clinging to any thread, Anous pointed at Raouf. "I maintained a pure friendship!" he claimed.

"Did you not ultimately kill it off brutally?"

"I suffered enormous sadness afterward," said Anous.

"That is uncontestable," admitted Abu.

"And what of my love for cats and my tenderness toward them?"

"That, too, is beautiful."

Abu reflected for a moment, then resumed his interrogation. "What was your attitude toward your father's tyranny?"

"I was just a dutiful son!"

"Such devotion was hardly appropriate in a case like yours."

"Some of his actions always disgusted me."

"Yet you greatly admired other things he did that were no less appalling."

"If only I had lived long enough to change all that. . . ."

"You are being tried for what was, not for what might have been."

". . . Or if I could be given another chance."

"Perhaps that could be arranged," mused Abu.

"When will I appear in court?"

"Your trial is already concluded," replied Abu solemnly. "Anous Qadri, I regret to inform you that you have been condemned."

At these words, like a wisp of fog in the rays of the sun, Anous vanished into the void.

Raouf gazed at Abu questioningly. "Will I continue as his spiritual guide?"

"He will not be reborn on earth for at least a year, or perhaps even longer."

"What then, will my new assignment be?" wondered Raouf.

Mournfully, Abu told him, "You must present yourself for trial once again."

"Did I not put every effort into it?"

"Indeed, you did, but you failed. Your man was condemned, as you have seen."

"The important thing is the work, not the result."

"The work and the result are both important," Abu admonished. "Moreover, you made a monstrous mistake."

"What was that, Abu?"

"It was not your mission to make him confess to killing you, as though that had been the only or the biggest crime in your quarter."

"But wasn't that his main problem?"

"No," said Abu.

"What was it, then?"

"His father was the problem," Abu advised. "If you had goaded him against his father, then you would have attained higher goals!"

Raouf fell into a pained silence as Abu continued to lecture him, "You did not choose the right target. Your egoism got the better of you, though you did not know it. It would have been easier to provoke him to rebel against his father. If he had succeeded in that, he would not have been disgraced. But it was hardly easy for a foolish, pampered young man to sacrifice his own life—while his father's felonies included your murder."

"Please tell me the verdict," Raouf said in resignation.

"Raouf Abd-Rabbuh, I regret to inform you that you have been condemned."

As soon as Abu pronounced his sentence, Raouf, too, was gone.

14

There was a lengthy inquiry into the case of Rashida Sulayman. She went to trial, where she convinced the court that she had acted in self-defense. The result was acquittal. Her mother decided that to remain in the *hara* at the mercy of Boss Qadri the Butcher posed an unpredictable danger, so she fled that night with her daughter, destination unknown.

At the same time, the bursting stream of life in the alley began to wash away the froth of sadness. Raouf's destitute mother married Shaykh Shakir al-Durzi six months after the death of his wife. She bore him a son that she named Raouf to immortalize the memory of the one she had lost. Yet this was not really Raouf returning, but the soul of Anous in a new guise. Likewise, one of Boss Qadri's wives gave birth to a boy that the father called Anous, in honor of the son taken from him—but this was none other than Raouf's spirit transmigrated to a new body.

15

The child Raouf (Anous) grew up in the house of Shakir al-Durzi, along with many brothers and sisters, in a life of luxury, thanks to the bribes that Qadri the Butcher paid the shaykh of the alley. Yet the shaykh did not preoccupy himself with raising his children, or with marrying off his daughters. None of the boys were educated beyond Qur'an school, but worked in the lowest trades, whether in the *hara* itself or outside it. Nor was Raouf more fortunate than his brothers. At the beginning, his mother insisted that he excel in learning, only to be harshly reprimanded by her husband. Soon the boy was given a petty job in a bakery. Raouf was glad for that, because he did not find within himself either the true inclination or drive to study. As he grew older he understood the actual situation in his alley—the cocky dominance of Boss Qadri the Butcher, and the despicable role played by his father. And there was the life of poverty to which he was fated, in the service of Rashad al-Dabash, the bakery's owner.

Anous (Raouf) had been his classmate at school. They had a natural sympathy for each other, and spent all their time playing together. A strong bond of affection was forged between them. Nonetheless, life separated them despite their living in the same quarter. Anous was enrolled in primary school after Qur'an school, then in secondary school, before finally entering the Police Academy. Perhaps they sometimes met on the street, or in the home of Qadri the Butcher when Raouf was delivering dough or returning with loaves of bread. At such times they would each exchange a fleeting smile, or a greeting—from Anous' side—that seemed a bit feeble. Raouf could tell that their childhood friendship was dwindling away and evaporating, and their two worlds were growing further and further apart. He felt more and more sharply the contradictions of life, and its miseries. He was annoyed with Anous, but he utterly loathed Qadri the Butcher and Rashad the Baker, and abhorred his own father. Indeed, the flame of life singed him, kindled by what he heard that the young people were saying in the coffeehouse—until Anous himself would sit with those same youths, expressing his views with passion. With this he appeared to be a strange young man, at odds with the house in which he dwelt, in rebellion against his infamous father.

For his part, Boss Qadri the Butcher watched Anous's development with unease. This was a peculiarly peevish offspring, one that stirred fears; he even once called him "a bastard son."

One day he asked him, "What do you say to the riffraff in the café, and what do they tell you?"

"We exchange our concerns, father," he answered politely.

"They are your enemies," objected Qadri.

"They are my friends," Anous said, smiling.

"If you overstep your limits, you'll find me another person, without any mercy whatsoever," swore Boss Qadri.

Qadri told himself that soon his son would become a police officer. Then he would become mature and know his place in life. Next, he would marry—and his problem with him would end.

Anous did indeed graduate as an officer. He was appointed to their own quarter through his father's influence and his courting of highly placed persons.

16

Time is what made Raouf and Anous turn out differently than expected. A current swept through the alley, or rather new currents did—both rebellious and even revolutionary. And so they burst out of the suffocating air at home, each one adopting a new personality. No one sensed the danger from Anous before he became a policeman. Yes, there had been alienating disturbances between himself and his father, yet Qadri had thought everything would change in his favor when his son was officially launched in his career.

As for Raouf, his employer, Rashad al-Dabash, soon grew angry with him. He slapped him on the face, shouting, "Look out for yourself—and don't lead your pals down the wrong path!"

If it weren't for his father Shakir al-Durzi's rank as shaykh of the *hara*, then Raouf would have lost his job, though Rashad complained to him about the boy. The shaykh was astounded at this new type of insubordination, and sought to tame him with a harsh beating. When he found him still stubborn, he resorted to calling on the officer.

"*Effendim*," Anous advised, "threaten him with the law—that is better than our having to arrest him tomorrow."

Thus Raouf appeared before his old friend Anous. For a long time they traded just looks with each other, then memories they shared together, until their faces glowed with the warmth of their old camaraderie.

"How are you, Raouf?" Anous asked him, smiling.

"Miserable," Raouf replied, "so far away from you."

"You should have continued your education," Anous told him.

"That was my father's doing—and what's done is done."

"Look out for yourself," Anous told him seriously. "The law has no mercy."

"The Boss caused all this evil—and there's no mercy in his heart."

Lowering his voice, Anous repeated, "Watch out for yourself. . . ."

After this, Anous sought to shake up the *hara*'s consciousness, and to make his father tremble. He had Shaykh Shakir al-Durzi transferred to another alley, putting a new, more trustworthy man, Badran Khalifa, in his place. This hit Boss Qadri the Butcher like a violent revolution, depriving him of the precious right hand that had shielded him from the law.

"How did this happen when you're an officer in the station here?" he confronted his son.

"That protection is for you—and the people too."

"You're my son—and my enemy, Anous."

"Know, father, that I'm your faithful son."

Each speaking their own language, mutual comprehension between the two became impossible, and black dust covered the house's face.

17

A woman came to meet Anous in the station. When his eyes beheld her face, his breast was moved by a sweet new melody. Such a wonder, this serene beauty with her dark, almond-shaped eyes. It was as though her image was already engraved in his passion to awaken it anew. She was at least twenty years older than he was: her expression entwined serenity and sadness.

"I've come to request your protection," she told him.

"What is your name?" asked Anous.

"Rashida Sulayman, schoolteacher," she told him. "Recently, I was transferred to the New Era School in this quarter."

That name—hadn't it flitted before through the tangle of his memory?

"Whom do you fear?" he queried her, his eyes fixed on her face with infatuation.

"It's ancient history," replied Rashida. "I may be exposed to an attack on my life because of it."

"Really?" he said raptly. "What's the history? And who would the attacker be?"

"It's an old legal issue in which I was found innocent—a case of self-defense," she explained. "But the father of the person killed is a frightful man with many criminal supporters."

The old story that he had heard repeatedly in his childhood assailed him like a sudden storm. Shaken, he struggled to control his battered nerves. Standing before him was the woman who had killed his brother, the first Anous. Had she beguiled him the way she had bewitched his brother before him?

"We ran away to Imbaba," she continued her tale. "I trained to be a teacher in the provinces, until I was suddenly transferred to our old neighborhood."

He fell silent, caught up in the vortex of his emotions. He had not asked her the name of the person she feared—but then she said, "The man is well-known to everyone here: Boss Qadri the Butcher."

"Are you married, ma'am?" he queried, steadying himself with an enormous effort.

"I have never wed," she told him.

"Why haven't you explained your circumstances to the school administration in this district?"

"No one would pay any attention to me."

"Where do you live?"

"At 15 al-Durri Street, Imbaba."

"Stay calm," he told her. "I will speak to the administration myself. And if it takes a while to get results, then I will see to your protection personally."

"Thank you," she said warmly. "Please don't forget me!"

No, he would not be able to forget her.

18

Anous found no difficulty in annulling her transfer. He went by himself to the house at 15 al-Durri Street in Imbaba. The time was late afternoon. The Nile seemed still, cool fires gliding along its surface. Rashida received him with surprise blended with pleasure and hope, then guided him into her small, well-furnished sitting room.

"Please excuse my stopping by," he said, "but I wanted to put your mind at ease immediately. I was able to undo your move at work."

"A thousand thanks to you, *effendim*!"

She ordered coffee for him, thus offering him a chance to tarry, as he had hoped.

"Do you live with your mother?" he asked her.

"My mother passed away ten years ago," she replied. "I have no one but an old woman who is my faithful housekeeper."

What a shame that Rashida is a spinster, though she still retains her beauty.

"Would it disturb you to know that I am Anous Qadri, son of that same terrifying butcher?"

Rashida was shocked. Her brown face flushed, its expression changed completely—yet she said not a word.

"I have upset you," he fretted.

"I'm just surprised," she said tremblingly.

"Please don't hate me," he begged.

"You're just a normal person," she said shyly.

He continued sipping his coffee while drinking in glances he stole at Rashida. Then he laughed nervously, "I'm not frightening like my father!"

"I'm sure of that," she said.

"Really?"

"That's very clear—and the truth is, I'm innocent," she declared.

"And I'm sure of that," Anous affirmed. After a moment, he added, "But there is something that perplexes me."

She looked at him questioningly.

"Why haven't you married?" he asked.

She stared in the distance for a while, then answered, "I have refused more than one proposal."

"But why?"

"I don't know."

"Because of your love for the other man?"

"But that has been forgotten, like everything else."

"There must be a reason," he pressed her.

"The loss of my virginity was no small matter," she said. "Perhaps I have despaired of making anyone happy."

"That's a very regrettable thing," he said.

"Maybe it was meant to be," she said resignedly.

She's still a ravishing woman!

On his way home, Anous felt he was floating through an ethereal atmosphere. He loathed the duty that took him away from the house at 15 al-Durri Street in Imbaba.

It's true, I have fallen in love with Rashida.

19

Estrangement fell like a forbidding barrier between father and son. The mother was saddened to the point of death. The house became downcast, as oppressive as a rat's nest. Should he seek a transfer to one of the provinces? And what about Imbaba? What would happen if his father knew the passions burning in his breast? An unexpected thought occurred to him: he had been born as a punishment for his father. If not, why had he declared a secret war upon him from his earliest awareness of his surroundings? What a father deserving of absolute rejection, a sad and regretful situation—especially as I love the man totally. Though beastly and crude to the outside world, he is mild and kind inside his own home. He cannot picture his own perversity, believing instead that he is only exercising his natural right—the right of the smart and the strong. His greed for money and power knows no limits. As accustomed to committing crime as to saying good morning, he is solicitous to his supporters, generous to the point of profligacy. But when it comes to the common laborers, whose money he steals and whose food he hoards, Qadri scorns them all—without mercy. One day Anous will detest him so much that he will even deny the man is his father. Even more calamitous than this, the Boss has stamped Anous' mother with his character, for she worships his power. Every time he commits some outrage, she falls into raptures of adoration. Truly, he—Anous—dwells in the lion's den, in the temple of might and sin.

As things became more and more complicated, provocative situations emerged. He arrested his father's supporters as they were pilfering the money of the bakery's employees. No sooner had he locked them up—for the first time in the *hara*'s history—than a torrent of giddy joy exploded in the alley, stirring a volcano in the house of Boss Qadri the Butcher. No longer able to remain, Anous decided to go. His mother's torso shook as she wept.

"He is the Devil himself," she cried.

Anous kissed her forehead and left. He rented a small apartment in Imbaba, telling himself that putting an end to the activities of his father's supporters would do the same to his malignant powers. Qadri would be incapable of doing any more harm, and the quarter would slip from his hellish grip. He appealed to God, if only he could arrest his father in the very act of perpetrating a crime directly. Yet it appears that Qadri had resolved to meet the challenge with a similar one before his whole edifice collapsed—for on the same night a battle broke out between his supporters and the bakery's workers. During it, Raouf received a fatal wound. But before drawing his last breath, he managed to assassinate Boss Qadri the Butcher.

These were explosive events in rapid succession, shaking the *hara* to its very foundations, drowning it in blood—while dissipating the darkness that had engulfed it for so long.

20

The Butcher found himself in front of Abu, hearing him say, "Welcome, Qadri, to the First Heaven."

Acquainting the arrival with the place himself, he noticed that Qadri was absent-minded, with a dazed, faraway gaze.

"It seems as though you have not yet cut your ties to the earth," Abu pointed out to him.

"Something weighs heavily inside me," Qadri replied.

"Be aware—you will now learn your destiny."

"Yes, but I never imagined I would be killed by a mere boy like Raouf."

"Your new memory has not awakened yet."

Confusion showed in the furrows of Boss Qadri the Butcher's face. Slowly, slowly, he began to remember, until he let out a deep sigh.

"Do you recall now who this boy Raouf is?" Abu asked, smiling.

"My son Anous killed me," said Qadri painfully.

"Indeed," said Abu. "And do you remember who you were before that?"

"Adolf Hitler!" answered Qadri.

"And before that?"

"A notorious highwayman in Afghanistan. I can't even pronounce his name!"

"A long, black record," Abu upbraided him. "Why do you resist all advancement and waste every opportunity granted to you? Your son is better than you—many others are better than you."

"The lesson won't be in vain this time!" Qadri pleaded contritely.

"And yet, even as you appear before me now, you still have not left your worldly instincts behind!" Abu cajoled him.

"Perhaps I'm still stoned," said Qadri lamely.

"Your excuse is worse than the offense."

"I hope I can be made a guide. . . ."

"Do you have anything to say in favor of your behavior on earth?"

"Yes, I do," said Qadri. "I started out as an honest merchant. What made me greedy was other people's weakness, their carelessness, and their hypocrisy. Being a tyrant was fun for me, and there was nothing to stop me."

"The others will be punished for their weakness, just as you will be for exploiting it."

"Won't my murder at the hands of my own son count at all against my evil?"

"Such relations have no meaning here," snapped Abu. "How many sons and daughters have you killed, without even thinking about it?"

"Even so, I didn't create my own character, or my instincts."

"You own them freely," rebutted Abu. "In your freedom, you found no limits."

"If you improve your defense of me, then you can have anything you want," Qadri dangled.

"You are still clinging to the world," Abu laughed. "That is the most unforgivable sin of all."

"What do you say about my trial?"

"The trial is finished, Qadri," Abu disclosed. "You have been condemned."

And Qadri the Butcher was no longer there.

21

Raouf encountered Abu ensconced in his white cloud. There was a brief moment of mutual recognition, then a questioning look started to show in Raouf's eyes.

"Welcome to the First Heaven," said Abu.

He began to lecture Raouf for the usual orientation, then asked him, "How did you come to be here?"

"I was killed in a fight," replied Raouf.

"But you killed your killer, as well."

"I struck him while I was being stabbed," said Raouf. "I don't recall anything after that."

"For the second time, you arrive as both a killer and a person killed."

"Really?"

"I speak with some authority."

"What did I get the last time?" wondered Raouf.

"You were condemned," said Abu.

"Will that happen again now?" Raouf asked with worry.

"What would you like?" Abu asked.

"I rushed bravely into a just battle, and slew the Satan of our alley."

"That is true," conceded Abu.

His face jubilant, Raouf queried, "Is there hope for my acquittal?"

"Your negligence in the search for knowledge will count against you."

"But the circumstances I lived in were so extreme!"

"That is also true," said Abu. "But we evaluate the individual according to his struggle against his surroundings."

As the pain began to appear in Raouf's face, Abu told him, "You are a fine young man, but the ascent to the Second Heaven is a formidable feat indeed."

"Doesn't what I have done speak on my behalf?"

"Everything has been heard," answered Abu. "The verdict has been issued: you are appointed as a spiritual guide."

Raouf greeted the judgment with satisfaction, then Abu added, "More good news: you will be guiding Anous."

"The policeman?"

"Yes, his behavior bodes well for the ultimate result."

"Could that be the promised Paradise?"

Abu grinned as he replied, "There are seven heavens consecrated in service to the people of earth; but the time has not yet come to think about Paradise!"

"How does one climb from heaven to heaven?"

"Through the succeeding levels of judgment."

Perplexed, Raouf asked, "Shall we be spared further strife in the Seventh Heaven?"

"That is what customarily is said to give one hope and consolation," expounded Abu, still smiling, "though there is not one shred of evidence that it is true."

Streams of lyrical bliss flowed by, immersing them both in the waves of dripping pale clouds that spread over the endless expanse of verdure below.

The Disturbing Occurrences

———

I

l will always remember what I lived through during the horrific events in the al-Khalifa quarter of Cairo. To be sure, they weren't all horrific. Some were tales told of bags of money delivered to the homes of paupers in the dead of night. Others, though, involved mass poisonings, fires, and worse. Yet the fact each was done with the same modus operandi indicated that one person lurked behind them all. Everyone's eyes were on the lookout; all guards were on watch, as we ran organized patrols after dark throughout the district.

"This criminal is crazy—there's no doubt about that," I said to my chief.

"All that matters is we catch him," he answered sharply.

As the days of our search rolled on, I was utterly miserable—for we had no results, could find no leads at all—without any halt to the incidents themselves.

Then a letter came to me, with no signature, and only one line of writing:

The villain behind the crimes in al-Khalifa is Makram Abd al-Qayyum, who lives in the Paradise Building, Apt. 3.

Without hesitation we decided to put this man under observation. But just as quickly we learned he'd vacated his flat two days before. Immediately we launched an inquiry about him in the building. I met the owner, who also resided there.

"I want to hear everything you know about Makram Abd al-Qayyum, who lived in apartment three," I told him.

"He moved out two days ago," the man replied.

"I know that—but where did he move to?"

"Of that, he didn't inform me."

"Maybe you know where he sent the furniture that he'd brought with him?"

"The apartment's furnished," said the landlord. "He just took his bags out to the taxi and left."

"Did you recognize the taxi or the driver?"

"No."

"How old would you say he is?"

"Based on the way he looks and his health, it would be hard to say exactly—but I'd guess he's in his thirties or forties."

"What does he do for a living?"

"He's from the upper class. Yet he's very busy. He left

the building early each morning, returning at nightfall. Still, I never kept track of his movements except when my own happened to cross them."

"And his family?"

"He was alone. No one came to see him, so far as I know."

"And how were his dealings with people?" I pressed him.

"From my point of view, they were perfect," the man insisted. "He was a faithful renter, always paid his 200 pounds on the first of every month. He gave me absolutely no trouble at all."

"What about his personal behavior?"

"To my knowledge, it was beyond reproach. He displayed self-respect in every sense of the term."

"Didn't you know him well?"

"No," the owner said. "We met once to draw up the contract, and again to dissolve it—that's all."

"Any idea about his financial situation?"

"No, but he certainly seemed solvent. And he was spending 200 pounds for the apartment each month."

"He gave you no impression of being a queer, say, or a criminal?"

"He was as far away from all that as you can get."

"Describe his appearance for me."

"Tall, brawny, and well-built. Tawny-colored skin, with strong, well-defined features. A very elegant man."

"Any unusual characteristics?"

"Though his skin is dark, his hair and his mustache are both golden blond."

"How did he come to rent the apartment?"

"By way of Azuz, the flat-finder at the start of our street."

2

Finding few clues in the landlord's statements, I decided to try the doorman. He was a Nubian—as usual—but getting on in years.

"I'd like to talk about Makram Abd al-Qayyum," I told him.

"May God preserve him!" he replied.

"It seems that you like him."

"How could I not? He's the best of God's creatures."

Straightaway I asked about the taxi that hauled away the suspect's bags.

"The driver wasn't unknown to me," he answered.

I made a special note of this, then queried, "You said he was the best of God's creatures?"

"He never asked me to do any task without giving me a tip, and not just for the grand occasions and holidays. And he was always smiling; always greeting me whether coming or going, asking how I was doing. I'll never forget how he helped me when I was preparing my daughter for marriage. He's a dream for the deprived, and a balm for the wounded."

"I suppose that he informed you of where he was moving to?"

"No, but he told me he'd be passing by to see me often."

"You mean, to visit you particularly?"

"Perhaps when he comes to this district for one reason or another."

"Do you know why he changed his residence?"

"When I asked him about that, he said that he loves to wander."

"What do you think of his looks?"

"Strong, fearsome, and handsome. At the same time he was emotionally sensitive in a way that didn't at all match his powerful physique. Once, when he heard wailing over a dead person in our building, his eyes filled with tears. He used to give me money to buy bread for the stray cats that hung around the place. He was so gentle that he would toss peanuts into the stairwell for the mice that scurried there."

"All that is very nice," I said. "But you undoubtedly know things that no one else does about his personal behavior. A single man doesn't rent a furnished apartment for no reason at all."

"Absolutely no one else entered his flat," the Nubian insisted. "This is an aspect I couldn't miss."

"No friends and no relatives?"

"No friends, and no relatives."

"He was out all day?" I asked.

"From time to time he would eat lunch in his apartment. He'd order food from one of the local restaurants."

"Nothing inside his flat caught your eye?"

"I never went into his apartment."

"What do you know about the time he normally returned to his flat in the evening?"

"He most often came home about ten in the evening. He would then stay up till midnight or even dawn."

"What if someday it were proved to you that he poisoned innocent people and went around setting deadly fires?"

Startled, the man exclaimed, "That would be a warning that the gates of Hell have opened!"

3

We rounded up all the taxi drivers in the district and filed them before the doorkeeper. He recognized one of them, called Yunis, who the doorman said was the owner of the taxi that carried away Makram Abd al-Qayyum's bags. The driver had no difficulty remembering the fare: he said that he'd dropped him directly at the Semiramis Hotel.

I set off instantly to the Semiramis with a bunch of assistants. I was able to verify that the suspect spent one night in the place, leaving early the next morning. I asked about the taxi that took him away—and the porter told me that he carried his bags to a white, privately-owned Mercedes. The big, dusky, distinguished-looking gentleman with the golden hair drove the car himself. No one could remember its license number.

Is he the car's owner? If so, then why didn't he use it the whole time he lived in the Paradise Building? Did he buy it just yesterday? The more that I cut through the obscure character of his actions, the more the insinuation of his guilt took root inside me, and the instincts to investigate and take up the challenge became more deeply fixed within me.

4

After that I went to the neighbors living on the same floor in his building. The first was an architect named Raouf. He'd barely heard me utter the name of Makram Abd al-Qayyum when he began to scowl.

"Evidently, you don't find him too agreeable," I ventured.

"Damn him, he's a strange man," Raouf raged. "So wrapped up in himself that he's practically perverted. I wouldn't doubt that he hates all humanity."

"The doorman has another view of him entirely," I rejoined.

"Pay no attention to what the doorman says; a tiny gratuity makes his head spin. I'll never forget once when I met Abd al-Qayyum at the building's entrance. As I began to greet him he replied with a curt haughtiness—my heart sank and my blood boiled. He's impudent and ill-mannered."

"What you're saying is new to me."

"I challenge you to find one resident in this building who ever exchanged greetings with him. He's an arrogant crackpot. As for his cruelty . . ."

"Did you say, 'his cruelty'?"

"My wife told me that she saw him kick a cat," Raouf went on, "that he found in front of his apartment. The poor thing smashed violently against the wall, before it landed somewhere between life and death!"

"That's very strange!" I gasped.

"When a wake was held at the building he neglected

his human obligations without concern. He passed by the mourning tent, paying no attention to it whatsoever, nor did he acknowledge anyone there."

"What about his personal behavior? I mean, the furnished apartment . . ."

"No, no—no one visited him so far as I know. His type suffers from a hidden inadequacy that turns them into supercilious snobs."

"But he was well-off, or so it seems."

"Why not?" he asked. "Are there bigger bastards than the rich?"

5

This had surpassed mere suspicion—it was becoming a full-scale indictment. The doorman was credible, so was Raouf. My rock-solid familiarity with these crimes' history led me to this view. Who other than Makram Abd al-Qayyum would throw money onto the balconies of the poor, while planting poison in chocolates meant for innocents? Isn't he the one who provided money to feed stray cats, then kicked one of them to death without mercy?

I approached the second neighbor, an Arabic language instructor named Abd al-Rahman.

"The man lives alone, all right—but insolent, he's not. The problem is that Engineer Raouf hated him because he reacted dryly to his greeting—but maybe his mind was simply troubled at the time."

"And how do you see him?"

"I can testify to his piety," said Abd al-Rahman. "We always meet in the mosque at Friday prayers."

"Really?"

"I walked with him once after the prayers and found him very charming. He invited me to lunch at the Kursaal Restaurant downtown. He was so insistent that I could hardly get a word in edgewise. He told me of his enormous love for our religious heritage, and that he wanted my help to become more knowledgeable of it."

"Perhaps he's not well-educated."

"No, he's not exactly erudite in that field, but he did graduate from the College of Law, and studied law and history in the Sorbonne."

"Maybe you're the first to mix with him," I suggested.

"Maybe I am, but we used to meet at the bar in the Mena House Hotel by the Great Pyramid. To me it was clear he had a lot of friends there—both Egyptians and foreigners. He was called to the phone so often, I thought he must be in business."

"It never occurred to you to ask him about his occupation?"

"Once I asked him a bit craftily about how he spent his time. He answered that he loved innumerable things, yet he was not committed to any particular kind of work. In other words, he's rich."

"What's the source of his wealth?"

"Land, stocks and bonds, and so on," Abd al-Rahman replied. "Yet his greatest asset is that he is quite well read. At one point I proposed to him that he write history, and he smiled and asked me, 'Do you think there's really such a thing as history?' I thought he was just kidding, but he saw this and said, 'To get rich on history comes through praise, and on poetry through libel.'"

"Of course, you don't know why he has avoided marriage?"

"Once I complained to him that one of my sons was acting up," he said. "Makram told me with a sadness that seemed unusual for him, 'A son's rebellion means endless sorrow.' The ring of anguish in his voice told me he was that son, or perhaps even the afflicted father himself. Rather slyly I said, 'You've released yourself from all that.' He looked at me and smiled—but without sating my curiosity."

"Why didn't you clarify this point?" I goaded him.

"I was close to him—I even revered him. I was afraid I'd lose him by putting too much pressure on him."

"Naturally, he let you know that he intended to leave."

"Never . . . his departure surprised me. But I'll surely be seeing him on Thursday at the Mena House."

"I don't think so. In any case, we'll see."

"Why do you say, 'I don't think so'?"

"Don't you know that he's suspected of being behind the disturbing occurrences in our area?"

The man's eyes widened in dismay as he said—not only incredulously, but in protest—"I seek refuge in God from the accursed Satan."

6

The mystery grew murkier, merging into darkness, but my intuition—honed by years of experience—became conviction, or nearly so. I was just about fully satisfied with my conclusions, based on the information gathered by that time, and was ready to speed up the pursuit. But I saw no harm in meeting the third resident. This was Makram Abd al-Qayyum's next-door neighbor, the tax collector, Bakr al-Hamadhani.

The tax man had hardly heard the suspect's name when he blurted, "The madman!"

"Mad?"

"Of course! Every time I heard his voice it was reverberating like a drum in the quiet of the night. Was he talking on the telephone? To himself? Was he having an imaginary fight? You'd think it was a blast of wind or a rumble of thunder. And there was something else really astonishing."

"Really?" I mused.

"He would sing and play the oud."

"This is something new indeed."

"His voice is actually strong and beautiful. Sometimes he sang songs of the utmost dignity, like, 'Oh how I long to see you.' But other times they were tunes of the most extreme banality, like, 'Now I'm a teacher, I used to be a fool.' Just imagine this somber man crooning, 'The day you bit me so hard.' He was such a raucous fellow.

"One time I was returning from an evening at the theater, and saw him outside the Vladimir Tavern, staggering drunk. 'Bring it on!' he shouted, slurring his words."

"So he was rowdy?"

"How strange that was! But there were stranger things, too. One night as I came home from my evening out I saw him walking a few steps ahead of me. He went into his flat and I headed toward mine. For some reason, I noticed that the peephole on his door was open. I took a peek through it and, at the end of the foyer, I could see a well-lit room, perhaps a sitting room. But the bizarreness of what I saw nailed me where I stood.

"I saw it contained a whole variety of marvels. On the wall facing me strange masks were hung, both beautiful and ugly, along with the heads of stuffed animals. Also weapons from various historical periods, along with musical instruments. And in the center of the room there was what looked like a fully-stocked chemical laboratory."

"A chemical laboratory?"

"Yes, a long table on which glass vials full of various-colored liquids were arrayed, long canisters mounted on metal bases, crucibles, power generators."

"Amazing," I muttered. "Simply amazing."

"I went to my flat flabbergasted. I woke up my wife and told her what I saw. She accused me of being intoxicated. I dared her to come out with me to see for herself . . . an extraordinary sight."

"Did you ever say hello to each other or have a conversation?"

"Not once. Honestly, I was afraid of him. I recited 'There is no god but God' when I heard he'd gone away."

7

The same day I paid a visit to Azuz, the flat rental agent. I no longer needed new information on the suspect's personality, but I hoped to find a thread that could lead us to him. I found the man remembered the precise interaction between them, despite the passage of nearly a year.

"I could never forget that day," he declared.

"Why is that?"

"The bargaining was done in a minute. In fact, there was no bargaining at all. He was generous to an uncanny degree. But on the same day, I discovered that my billfold was missing. That's why it was a day I can never forget."

"How did that happen?"

"He handed me the cash and I put it on the desk, then he left. I was distracted for a moment by a telephone call. Then I picked up the money to put it in my wallet—but discovered that the wallet was gone without a trace."

"What was running through your mind?"

"The billfold had been with me. The only ones who entered my shop had been Makram Abd al-Qayyum, and the shoeshine man. At the time, my suspicion fell on the bootblack. I called him inside and questioned him; I was so harsh with him that he screamed. But he swore by the most sacred oath that he was innocent, and started crying."

"Of course, you didn't suspect the other?"

"No, sometimes I would be assailed by suspicions, but these were hard to establish. It burned me up to lose more than two hundred *gunayh*—but how could I level an accusation against someone like him? He was a man of influence, without the slightest doubt. What good would it do me to accuse him, except to bring his power down on my head?"

"So you surrendered this matter to God?"

"As happens in most cases of pickpocketing. But I would see him sometimes when he went out in the morning and mutter to myself, 'Our Lord is a mighty avenger.'"

8

That evening I met with my boss. I showed him the reports I had written up in meticulous detail. He began to read them with his head propped on the palm of his hand until he'd finished them. Then he stared at me, frowning.

"We have to recollect the whole picture," he said. "There are unnerving events. Some poor people find bags stuffed with money on their balconies, left by an unnamed benefactor. Others discover safe-looking packets of sweets, only to learn that the candies are poisoned, causing the deaths of unsuspecting people. Children are reported missing. Fires break out in bars. This is on one hand.

"On the other hand, you receive a letter from an unknown person that points the finger at Makram Abd al-Qayyum. You investigate this man and come to me with a clutch of contradictions that are more like the weird happenings themselves. What do you think?"

"I've become totally convinced that he's the criminal we're seeking."

"Convinced?"

"That's my gut feeling," I affirmed.

"I'm only interested in either a smoking gun or a confession."

"Let's not ignore the fact, sir, that the incidents stopped when he went away."

"That period has been very short; it means nothing."

"And don't forget that we've become the talk of the town."

"His compulsiveness will betray him sooner or later . . . No doubt, he's deranged!" the chief declared.

"Deranged?" I challenged him. "Possibly—but it's just as likely he's a sane, clever dog with a concealed motive."

9

I set off on the chase with dauntless energy. The patrols and the lookouts were doubled. I distributed his description to every department, outlining a comprehensive course of action to the leaders and to those experienced with criminal circles. I knew, of course, that—for me personally— he had come to define my future, and my duty. The subject took control of both my waking mind and my dreams. I thought it over, and thought it over again, and decided to put off making an appeal through the newspapers and other media, at least for the time being.

10

While we were immersed in the search, a sudden bolt of lightning struck us from the blue. The press surprised us with news of events similar to those in our district—but this time, in the Delta town of Tanta. I rushed to Tanta without even seeking leave to go, and gave all the information I had to the responsible authorities there.

As we were drawing up a new plan of attack profiting primarily from our earlier experience, the newspapers came out with stories of yet more incidents in the southern city of Asyut. Sensing that these crimes had become a national scandal, I went there immediately. When I arrived I telephoned my boss to tell him my location.

"Where are you?" he shouted. "What is this blatant insubordination?"

I tried to explain the situation but he cut me off.

"Get back here immediately," he demanded. "The incidents have returned to our own district."

11

I had the idea to invite a famous artist to meet with me and the eyewitnesses. I asked him to draw an accurate picture of the enigmatic culprit based on the interviewees' statements.

"Don't give up until you're sure it's a faithful portrait," I ordered.

The media ran the picture asking anyone who recognized the subject to direct us to him. Citizens pointed us to more than one person: a village headman, a fishmonger, a luggage dealer. The image even resembled a certain powerful man of state. The uproar grew out of control until we were the laughingstock of comedians and pundits alike.

"The administration is going up in flames," the chief sighed to me.

"You can't fault our plan," I countered.

"He that we haven't sought has come to us, while he that we *have* sought has eluded us."

"Maybe he's in hiding, or in disguise."

"No doubt the incidents investigated in all these districts are not the work of just one man," the chief asserted.

"Perhaps he's the head of a gang?"

"The administration is going up in flames!" he cried again in despair.

I returned to my office, blind with rage. At the doorway I heard a sharp exchange between the hall guard and another man who wanted to come in and meet me.

"I have no time for anyone now," I blurted sternly.

In a loud, even voice, the other man declaimed, "I am Makram Abd al-Qayyum."

12

I seized him by the arm and we went into the room. We stood there face-to-face. I was panting as he asked with calm resentment, "What is the meaning of what you published in the papers?"

"Why didn't you come in immediately?" I asked in return, scanning him closely.

"I was at the Red Sea, a long way from the newspapers—or anything else."

A burning, pregnant silence fell between us until he resumed questioning me.

"What's the point of this ridiculous charge against me?"

"We'll see," I told him, seething with pique.

I decided to conduct the interrogation in my chief's office, under his supervision.

13

What should I say?

The man answered every question quickly, with a solid simplicity—yielding not one shred of evidence against him. We showed him to the families of the victims, the informants, and the aggrieved in every part of the quarter. No one had seen him, either by day or by night. We broadcast a message to the anonymous author of the letter that had accused him, to share whatever information they had with us—but no one replied. And so Makram Abd al-Qayyum left us with head held high, while I was dealt a devastating blow.

Yet, astoundingly, deep down, I couldn't shake the feeling that he was our man.

14

Of course, there had to be a sacrificial ram, so the Interior Ministry decided to transfer me to headquarters. I put the most qualified person I knew for the job in my place. Outraged at the whole situation, I presented my resignation, announcing that I planned to practice law. I continued to follow the wave of atrocities and the news of the investigation, anxious that my successor would succeed in nabbing the perpetrator. The sentiment, though shameful, was only natural.

And what did I know but one day Makram Abd al-Qayyum himself burst into my office. I stared at him in shock as he sat down before my desk.

"I've come to propose that you manage my business and legal affairs," he said.

The offer was so tempting, it was virtually impossible to refuse. Still, I asked him, "Why me exactly, when I've only worked as a lawyer for two years?"

"But you have great experience. And I count myself responsible to some degree for your resignation."

Jokingly, I shot back, "Is this some sort of schadenfreude?"

"I seek refuge in God," he rebutted gravely, "but there are only benevolent feelings behind it."

Thus I came to serve the estate of the worthy Makram Abd al-Qayyum!

15

I can testify that I found him worthy in every sense of the term—dignified, well-versed, and fine of speech; benign in his dealings with others; openhanded as well as openhearted. Perhaps my enthusiasm would falter at times, and I would ponder, "What if he catches me off-guard with one of his famous contradictions? Wouldn't it be better for me to stick to the side of caution?"

Yet my whispering devil within was disappointed. Abd

al-Qayyum's tendency to always seem to act for the good truly tweaked my conscience.

One morning, after he had finished reviewing some work I had prepared for him, he tilted back in his swivel chair and said, "Finally—they've decided to close the case by laying it against 'a person unknown.'"

"Let that be a slap to repay the one that struck me," I gloated maliciously.

"Not at all—you were on the wrong track," he said, with sweet tranquility.

"But . . . ," I tried to interject.

"It was a mistake to focus suspicion on me," he interrupted swiftly, "because of an absurd letter lacking even a signature."

"It wasn't because of the letter, but came out of a most unusual investigation!"

"By concentrating on me, you let the real criminal slip out of your hands!"

"Was it unreasonable to connect the testimony of the eyewitnesses to the exotic nature of these acts?"

"My dear professor! Is there a human being devoid of contradictions? What's so strange if I feed cats while kicking a sick one that attacked me? What's so peculiar if I grow friendly with one man, while shunning another due to his nasty character? And what's new when one is sober at a certain moment and then relaxes by drinking to excess the next? Does this mean that I would poison children and go around setting murderous fires?"

I kept silent, both wary and reflective at the same time. Then he continued, "By the same logic, my dear friend, the identical accusation could be directed at you."

"Me?" I chuckled.

"Why not?" he retorted. "The crimes continued despite the increased guard and heightened vigilance of the informers. How did the culprit penetrate the well-mined district? He must have been confident that no one from the security forces would have suspected him. Terrific. . . . Who could this be if not the man in charge of surveillance? In other words, *you*."

I laughed harder and taunted, "And the incidents in Tanta?"

"The incidents in Tanta definitely happened, and so did your trip to that city. Whether your travel there came before or after these phenomena, I have no idea!"

"Great," I said, still laughing. "But what was the motive for all this mayhem?"

"The same one that, buried deep within the criminal, you wore yourself out completely trying to uncover."

"To my mind, he's insane."

"And is it impossible that you're insane?"

"Have you found anything in my work to make you doubt my sanity?"

"There are different kinds of insanity," he said. "The crazy person is the last one to know."

I guffawed to prove my contempt, but his speech had hurt me. What hurt most was that he was serious, so much so that I imagined for a moment he was making an actual accusation not only against me, but against all humanity. Then he smiled, and the gleam returned to his broad countenance.

"We've settled that now," he said, adopting a new tone. "Let's get back to work."

What a perplexing person he is! Without any doubt, it's a remarkable coup to be managing his affairs—while his personality is far too sublime for any possible involvement in such monstrous crime.

Why, then, does the inner certainty that he is guilty never leave me?

Room No. 12

The hotel manager recalls, like a photo he can never forget, how one day a woman came to take a room for just twenty-four hours. The time was exactly 10:00 a.m. The sight of such a stunning member of the opposite sex approaching him, utterly unaccompanied, made him stare at her, intrigued. Equally unforgettable: she seemed a lady of formidable influence—obvious in the firmness of her build, the fineness of her features, and the sharpness of her gaze. She stopped at the front desk, standing bolt upright in her red gown and white hat. She had no personal identity card, and was neither employed nor married. Most likely she was divorced or a widow. Her name was Bahiga al-Dahabi, coming from Mansura in the Delta. The man recorded all the necessary information, before pointing her toward a bellhop. The bellhop walked ahead of her, carrying her bag—one heavier than he was used to, leading her to room number twelve in the little hotel.

The bellhop returned after a half an hour, an amazed look on his face. When the manager asked him what had happened, he replied, "She's a very eccentric woman."

"What do you mean?" the manager wondered.

The bellhop said that she'd asked him to strip the coverlet, blanket, and sheets from the bed and to put them in the corner of the room until nightfall. As for the bed itself, she requested that he move it outside the room altogether, with the excuse that she could not sleep so long as there was a space beneath her large enough to conceal a man. He told her that her fear was groundless, that there had never been any kind of incident in the hotel since its founding. But she insisted, so he bowed to her will.

"You should have come back to me immediately," said the manager.

The bellhop apologized, saying that while her request was peculiar, it did not exceed any of the duties the hotel was bound to fulfill. Then he resumed his story, that she had ordered him to open wide the doors of her wardrobe—and to keep them open. The bellhop could tell from her voice that she was afraid a stranger could hide within it if the wardrobe were closed. So he carried out her command, he said, smiling as he did so.

"The amazing part is that she seemed so strong and brave," remarked the manager.

He thought for a bit longer, then asked, "Did she cough up a tip?"

"A whole half-pound," bragged the bellhop.

"She's certainly not typical, but there's no harm in that," the manager replied.

"I was passing by her locked-up room on my way to the laundry, when I heard a voice speaking very excitedly inside," said the bellhop.

"But isn't she by herself?"

"Still, she was talking angrily and her voice kept getting louder, too."

"A lot of people do that," the manager said. "Just because you talk to yourself doesn't mean that you're crazy."

The bellhop shook his head without saying anything, so the manager asked him, "Were you able to make out anything she was saying?"

"No, except one expression: 'It's not important.'"

The manager signaled firmly that he wanted to end their discussion. Then, as he was writing in the register, he added to the bellhop, "Be ever more vigilant—that's our obligation, in any case."

Thunder sounded, and the manager looked at the sky through the window and found it thickly overcast with clouds. The weather was very cold, with occasional showers of rain. At exactly 1:00 p.m., the woman telephoned from room number twelve.

"May I order lunch?" she inquired.

"We have no food in the hotel, but there's a restaurant close by," the manager told her. "What would you like, ma'am?"

"Mixed vegetables with chicken," she answered, "plus rice with minced meat and onions, a kilogram of assorted kabab, a set of oriental salads, a loaf of bread grilled with lamb, soft pastries, and two oranges."

The manager ordered all that she requested. Yet he was astounded by how much food she'd wanted—especially the meat. That alone would have been enough for six persons!

"She's crazed not just with fear—but with gluttony, too," he said to himself. "Most likely she'll leave the hotel during the afternoon, and I'll be able to get a look inside her room."

The food arrived, and an hour later the man from the restaurant returned to collect the tray and china. The manager couldn't resist looking at the plates—and found them all licked clean, except for the remains of some bones and congealed sauce. He decided to put the whole business out of his mind, but nonetheless found that the woman—the strange way she looked and acted—kept pursuing him, pressing in upon his thoughts. He couldn't say that she was beautiful, yet she had a kind of force and attraction. There was something frightening about her, along with things that aroused curiosity and even submission. And though he'd seen her for the very first time that day, she'd left an impression of familiarity that comes only with faces that have embedded themselves in one's memory from days of old.

He saw a man and woman coming toward him. "Is Madam Bahiga al-Dahabi staying here?" the man queried.

The hotel manager answered in the affirmative, then telephoned to see if the lady would let the visitors go up to her room. Obviously, these people were from the upper crust, at least in terms of material wealth. The wind wailed powerfully, making the chandeliers dance in the hotel's small lobby. Then quickly another eight persons arrived—four men and four women—and repeated the same question.

"Is Ms. Bahiga al-Dahabi staying here?"

Again the manager telephoned to obtain the guest's permission. That being granted, the group mounted the stairs with a lofty air—they were from the same elevated crowd as the couple that preceded them—to room number twelve. There were now ten visitors in all—either relatives from one family, or friends, or friends and relatives combined. Whatever the case may be, there was no doubt that Madam Bahiga was no ordinary dame.

"Why did she choose our hotel?" he wondered.

Bustle spread through the establishment's bar as the staff carried tumblers of tea above, and it occurred to the manager that he had seen some of the faces in the second group before. But then he said to himself that the best thing would be to purge his brain of any thoughts of Bahiga al-Dahabi. Tomorrow she would be just another one of hundreds of lost memories that cluttered the humble hotel.

Then he found before him a woman of about fifty, possessing the ultimate in poise and comportment. "Is Madam Bahiga al-Dahabi in residence?"

When he said yes, she told him, "Tell her, if you please, that the lady doctor is here."

He contacted the madam, who said the physician could come up. Then he yielded to an insistent urge by asking before she left him, "What is your specialization, doctor?"

"Obstetrics," the woman replied.

He noticed that she had introduced herself with her professional title, but without her name. *Is she visiting the woman in that capacity? Is Bahiga al-Dahabi suffering from a feminine condition? Is she pregnant?* Yet he was not able to give full rein to his thoughts before a short, fat man with a scowling face marched in, introducing himself as Yusuf Qabil, contractor. He posed the much-repeated question, "Is Madam Bahiga al-Dahabi here?"

After the hotel manager had sought and obtained permission for the contractor to go up to her room, he bid the man goodbye with a perplexed and sarcastic smile. Meanwhile, one of the bellhops returned from an errand outside, shivering from the cold within his thick, rustic *gallabiya*. Darkness, he said, was gathering in the four corners of the sky, and soon the day would be turned into night. The manager glanced again out the window, but he was really thinking about the woman in room number twelve—the mysterious femme fatale with her top-drawer coterie. He began to feel that a current of unrest and unease had spread throughout the hotel since her arrival. It permeated his own inner being, arousing within him adolescent dreams of the languorous splendor of rich, worldly occupations.

He was jolted from his reverie by a voice asking, "Is Madam Bahiga al-Dahabi here?"

He beheld a big man wrapped in a jubbah and caftan, a tarboosh tilted back on his head, his hand gripping a gray umbrella. "Tell her that Blind Sayyid the Corpse Washer has come."

His chest heaving with revulsion, the manager gritted

his teeth, cursing the man and the woman both—but he did his duty by calling her. For the first time, he met a contrary response.

"Please wait in the lobby, sir," he told the undertaker.

What did he come to do here? Why doesn't he wait outside? The manager had worked in the hotel for fifty years, yet had never seen anything like what was happening that day. He was afraid that the rain would start coming down in torrents, keeping them all locked up inside the hotel for no one knew how long—and with this messenger of Death!

New visitors arrived. They came separately, but in succession: the owner of a furniture store, a grocer, a sugarcane juice vendor, the proprietor of a shop for cosmetics and perfumes, a high official in the Revenue Department, the editor of a well-known newspaper, a fish wholesaler, a procurer of furnished flats, an agent for an Arab millionaire. The manager thought the lady would move her meeting down to the lobby, but instead she kept granting permission for them to come up, one after the other. The bellhops brought them more and more tea and chairs, while the manager wondered how they could all find places to sit. Did they all know each other before? And what, exactly, had brought them together now? He summoned the head bellhop and asked him what he knew about these things.

"I don't know what's going in there," he answered. "Hands reach out to take the chairs and the tea inside, then the door closes again immediately."

The manager shrugged his shoulders. So long as no one

complained, he told himself, then he was not to blame for anything.

Blind Sayyid the Corpse Washer came up to him. "I'd like to remind the lady that I am here waiting," he said.

"She promised to call you at the appropriate time," the manager told him, with a feeling of futility.

The man wouldn't move, so he called the lady again, handing the mortician the telephone at her request.

"Madam, it's already past the afternoon prayer, and the days in winter are very short," he chided.

He bent into the receiver listening for a moment, then put it back and returned to the lobby, clearly disturbed. The manager damned him from his deepest heart. The woman was responsible for inviting this ghoul to the hotel, he thought as he glanced at the lobby's door with aversion and disgust. Meanwhile, some of the lady's guests came down on their way outside, and the manager's apprehensions about the goings-on in room number twelve seemed to lessen.

"Some of the visitors will go sooner and some later; they'll all be gone by nightfall," he assured himself.

He began to worry that his position of responsibility would force him into a confrontation with them—and they were from a powerful class. His dismay redoubled with the wind that whistled violently outdoors and the sense of distress that cloaked the roads. Yet despite these forbidding conditions, he saw a group of men and women wearing raincoats gathered at the door, and his heart sank in his chest. He surprised them by asking, "Madam Bahiga al-Dahabi?"

One of them, laughing, replied, "Tell her, if you please, that the delegates from the Association for Heritage Revival have arrived."

So he telephoned the woman, and as she gave her consent for them to come up he pleaded with her, "There are ten of them, madam, and the lobby downstairs is at your disposal for any number of visitors."

"There's plenty of space in the room," she retorted.

As the male and female delegates ascended, the manager shook his head in total confusion. *Sooner or later, there's going to be a clash.* The fury of heaven was about to descend outside—provoked by the assorted oddballs in room number twelve. The manager chanced to turn around to the lobby, and caught sight of Blind Sayyid the Corpse Washer creeping toward him. So he rapped the table with his knuckles in agitation, then put the man directly in touch with the woman by telephone before he could open his mouth. The manager listened to him complain to her, then heard him accede. The undertaker hung up the receiver by himself, but then grumbled as the manager began to walk away, "Waiting around with nothing to do is very boring."

The manager became enraged, and would have scolded him if the lady hadn't telephoned at that moment, asking to be connected to the restaurant. Her conversation with them continued for some minutes. Would she and her guests remain in the room until dinner, the manager pondered, and where would they dine? How he wished he could examine her room now: it had to be a scene beyond all imagining—an insane spectacle indeed.

While the torrent continued outside without any hint of slowing, a group of university professors and men of religion came—so immersed in deep discussion, that the manager simply let them go upstairs. The situation was becoming more and more nightmarish, as a mysterious man went up without first passing by the desk. The manager called out to the intruder—who did not respond. One of the bellhops followed him, but stopped when the man ducked into room number twelve. The manager now felt he was all alone, that he had lost fundamental control of the hotel. He considered summoning the head bellhop, but then a man appeared, the mere sight of whom brought him relief. They shook hands and the manager told him, "You've come at the right time, honorable informer, sir."

"Show me the register," the informer said calmly.

"Strange things are happening here," the manager blurted.

As the informer perused the names in the ledger, jotting down notes as he read, the manager said, "I suppose you've come because of room number twelve."

"Eh?" the informer coughed quizzically.

"Mad depravity is running riot in there," warned the manager.

"Anything found in nature must be natural," the informer said dismissively. Then, taking his leave, he said, "If anyone wants me on the phone, I'll be in room number twelve."

The manager became even more confused—yet at the same time, he was comforted to think that the government's eyes and ears knew what was happening in the hotel. He remembered that he was going to summon the head bellhop, and just as he pressed the ringer to call him, he observed Blind Sayyid once again slinking up to him. Losing his grip on his nerves, he shouted, "She told you to wait until she invited you up!"

The man grinned in habitual servility to the rebuke, then pleaded, "But I've been waiting so long. . . ."

"Wait without any backtalk—and remember you're in a hotel, not a boneyard!" the manager fumed.

The man retreated in feigned patience, as the manager recalled the head bellhop. "How are things going in room number twelve?" he queried.

"I don't know, but there's a lot of racket in there."

"How can they all squeeze into that place? They must be sitting on top of each other!" the manager marveled.

"I don't know any more than you do," the head bellhop mused. "In any case, the officer is inside with them."

The man wandered off as the manager went to look once more out the window, and saw the night weighing heavily in the void. The lights were on throughout the hotel, casting a wan radiance through the atmosphere thick with damp from the howling, raging wind outside. A battalion of waiters came from the restaurant, bearing trays crammed with all kinds of food, and the manager's astonishment grew. The room had only one dining table, so where would the woman's guests put all those plates? How could they consume their meals? One of the bellhops told him that the room's door no longer opened, and that the food only went in now through the little peep window.

What's more, the uproar from the room was afflicting

the entire hotel: the whole spectacle was now simply incredible.

After a half hour, the bellhop came back to confirm that the lot of them were drunk.

"But I haven't seen a single bottle go up there!" exclaimed the manager.

"Maybe they hid them in their pockets," the bellhop surmised. "They're singing, shouting and clapping—a case of drunken rowdiness, to be sure. And sinfulness too, for there's as many women as men in that room."

"And the informer?"

"I heard his voice singing, 'The World Is a Smoke and a Drink,'" said the bellhop.

Thunder boomed outside as the manager said to himself, "I could well be dreaming—and I could just as well have gone mad." At that instant, a group of common people approached—their faces and clothes proclaimed their low social status. They asked the inevitable question, "Is Ms. Bahiga al-Dahabi staying here?"

The manager smiled despairingly as he contacted the woman. She asked him to keep them waiting in the lobby and to serve them drinks as well. He pointed the way to the group of them and ordered the staff to give them tea. The lounge was overflowing, upsetting the undertaker. The manager again smiled hopelessly, muttering, "This hotel is no longer a hotel, and I'm no longer the manager, and today is not a day, and lunacy is laughing at us in the shape of meat and wine!"

The rain began to gush down again in sheets, and the sky to thunder. The asphalt at the hotel's entrance gleamed with the light of the electric lamps as feet scurried in from outside. The waiters all cried, "There is no god but God!" while the passersby took refuge in the foyer. The battering blows of the rain rattled the windowpanes without ceasing.

The manager left his post and went to the entrance, turning his face up to the blackened sky. Then he looked down at the water sluicing stones over the sloping ground. First the rain beat down, then it flared up with wrath, before detonating in a surging deluge over the hapless earth.

"There hasn't been rain like this for at least a generation," he declared.

Digging back in his past, he remembered a similar flood from his childhood. He recalled how it stopped all means of transport, blocking up the alleys and completely drowning rooms—and those in them—beneath porous roofs. He then went back to his desk, intent upon his work with the hotel records and expenditures, but he also issued orders to tighten the surveillance of the rooms and of the roof. He called for the head bellhop and asked him, "What news of room number twelve?"

"The singing and laughing show no sign of stopping," the man said, twisting his lips. "They're crazy in there!"

Blind Sayyid the undertaker loomed at the lobby's door.

"Get back to your place!" shrieked the manager.

The man held up his hand in entreaty, and the manager yelled at him once more, "Not another word!"

The thunder clapped like bombs as the massive rain pounded the pavements with incandescent intensity.

The manager mused that the old hotel wasn't built with reinforced concrete—and the night warned of yet more travails.

Another bellhop told him, "There are complaints in room number twelve about the leaky roof and the water pouring in."

"You mean they've stopped laughing and singing?" the manager demanded, exasperated. "Then let them all leave the room now!"

"But they can't!" protested the bellhop.

The manager dismissed him once again and called the head bellhop, asking him about what his assistant had said. "The rooms are all leaking, so I've mobilized all the men to plug the holes in the roof with sandbags."

"And what about room number twelve?"

"They're all jammed in there too tightly. Their stomachs have inflated so much, they can't open the door. They can't even move!"

Cosmic ire was smiting the night outside, while inside a frenzied air of activity filled the hotel as the bellhops scurried about with sandbags to halt the invading rain.

Then a most peculiar thing happened: the people who'd been waiting in the lobby rushed voluntarily to aid in the effort. The manager watched all this with delight—made greater by the fact that Blind Sayyid the Corpse Washer did not take part.

After a while the head bellhop reported on the work's progress. "They're putting all they've got into it," he said with pride. "But as for our friends in room number twelve, their condition is very bad—and getting worse and worse all the time."

What the man said struck the manager like a shock—
and amid the violent, pent-up tension of the entire day, he
snapped. His anger taking hold of his flesh, his blood,
and his nerves at once, he finally surrendered his last
shred of sanity.

"Listen." he said. "Remember exactly what I'm about
to tell you. . . ."

The bellhop stared at his face in terror as the manager
shouted with stark resolve, "Ignore room number twelve
and everyone in it!"

"Sir, the men are screaming and the women are crying!"

Bellowing like a beast, the manager railed, "Concentrate on the roof over the guest rooms—but as for room
number twelve, *leave it alone—and everyone inside it!*"

The bellhop tarried for merely a second, and the manager foamed with an even more animal-like fervor, "Carry
out my instructions to the letter—without dragging your
feet!"

He moved to face the window and watched the storm
crashing in the heart of the darkness, waxing more and
more perilous with each passing moment. Yet he felt his
great burden lighten, as his confidence returned with his
clarity of mind.

The Garden Passage

————

After long hesitation, I decided to go.

The curtain dropped at nightfall. Engulfed by the waves of gloom that swept Virgo Star Alley, I knew my path by the backlight of memory—the destroyer of darkness and the sojourner's guide. I squeezed through the iron gate that hung ajar, to be struck by the scent of a familiar incense. To my good fortune, I found no visitors in the house. She appeared to me alone, sitting cross-legged on her Persian divan, wrapped in a robe of many quiet colors embroidered with a pattern of crescent moons and flowers, drawn over the curves of a distinctly firm form. Her eyelids dangling like veils, in her fingertips she held some cards—she never grew bored peering into the Unseen on her own. She did not lift her eyes toward me, as though she knew who was coming by the sound of his footsteps, and as if she intended to pay him no heed. Sensing strongly that I was intruding, I did not offer her greetings, but sat in the chair nearest her, seeking refuge in silence. She continued reading her cards as I contemplated how to open our conversation, when all that I had prepared to say evaporated from my mind under the effect of this room, grave with the remains of days gone by. Suddenly she started, as though the cards had yielded an unusual revelation.

"I see a final assault upon his stubbornness!" she whispered.

She let out an "Oh!" of pleasure, muttering as she completed her vision, "A lead-tipped whip shall scourge his back!"

"What's passed has passed. I must look toward tomorrow," I said in recognition of her allusion to me.

"Your indulgence, my master!" she exclaimed, as though surprised by my presence.

"I came to settle my debts and to look toward tomorrow," I replied, putting a medium-size envelope in front of her.

"He came to settle his debts and to look toward tomorrow," she declaimed to her cards.

"Bread and salt have brought us together, and you are the mistress of those who know!"

Sounding straightforward at last, she replied, "Such things happen every day."

"This is the time for but one request," I said heatedly.

"Security," she said quietly.

"Security," I echoed, feeling encouraged. "Whenever I consult a friend on the matter, they always point to just one man."

Smiling, she replied, "He is the one who is always pointed to these days."

"As he is known for his hatred of intermediaries, I have not found anyone to intercede for me," I said with worry. "Yet they tell me that none of the great ever turn you aside."

"This is true, if they have been my companions," she admitted with pride.

Not knowing what to say, I simply sighed, when she said in a kindly tone, "You must find your own way."

"You're joking," I said, a sarcastic laugh escaping my lips.

"If only he came one time to his queen, like the others," she lamented. "Most of the patrons at the Moon Tavern are my minions—except for him."

"If only this miracle would occur!" I said wistfully.

We stared at each other for quite a while, until her eyes widened with a dawning insight. She giggled, then asked me, "What do you think?"

I gazed at her questioningly.

"You will undertake a mission," she declared.

"What mission?"

"That you bring him here to me."

"But how?"

"He leaves the Moon Tavern at midnight," she said. "Then he cuts through the Garden Passage to the square, where his car is waiting—the passage is the most fitting place for you to meet him."

"But he doesn't know me from Adam!"

"Use your manners as a man of good family to approach him," she said, drowning in laughter, "and whisper to him, 'Do you crave a tasty glass? A clean, well-hidden house?'"

I scowled as I turned my face away from her, seething with derision.

"My suggestion doesn't please you?" she asked.

"Mock my predicament all you want!"

Earnestly she rejoined, "I'm quite serious, if security is truly what you seek."

"How do you imagine I would accomplish that myself?" I bristled in annoyance.

"What is it but a fleeting adventure that flows from the search for what is sought?"

"Don't you have many who are professionals in that?" I asked, trying to hide my trepidation.

"I do not need any of them," she said with disdain.

"Yet I would be your first choice?"

"This is only an escapade—don't you understand?"

"No, I understand nothing."

"But it is your duty to understand," she scolded. "There's no harm if you pick a spot far from the lamplight, so the darkness might embolden you."

"And what about my dignity?"

"I'm not calling on you to make this your livelihood," she protested. "It's a one-time gambit. If you reject it, then you must know another way to reach your goal."

On my way back, I was so upset that I could scarcely see what was in front of me. I had absolutely no doubt about the power that woman held over men. Yet, driven by an angry, petulant resolve, I refused to submit, until I imagined that I was no longer obsessed with my quest for security—a person's last refuge when nothing else remains. It was as though I cared little about having to endure the demon of inflation, the ordeal of survival, the debasement of a time of deprivation. A merciless, ceaseless war broke out in my head. I kept wandering through the cafés and bars in a night that did not want to end. And not long before midnight I found myself standing in the Garden Passage in the furthest place away from the lamplight. What had brought me here? Perhaps I wanted to catch a glimpse from up close of that man whom I had seen only in the newspapers on momentous occasions.

He seemed to move with astral discipline—for at precisely the stroke of midnight his towering frame emerged from the Moon Tavern, tearing the silence with the tread of his heavy footsteps. My heart pounded as I tumbled from my lofty heights, and as he passed before me on his route to the square I took a step toward him. Immediately my mind was shattered by many terrors. I could almost feel the fingers pointed accusingly at me. My memory failed and my tongue froze. Abruptly aware that I was there, the man struck the ground with his cane to scold me for coming too near—so I quickly backed off, while he continued on his way.

All the next day I berated myself brutally. *Why did I go to the Garden Passage? Why did I try to approach that man?* And what kept me from speaking but my mind becoming scattered and falling prey to fears? The truth is that I am terrified of people—they are the ghosts that relentlessly pursue me. What good would they do me tomorrow, if the struggle to survive and the humiliation should grow even crueler?

I set off with great force to chase the strange things out of my life—and it never occurred to me that I would take up my position in the Garden Passage once again, just before midnight. Determined and confused, I waited until I found the man coming toward me on his course to the square. Drawing close to him, I whispered, "I have a cup and a lovely playmate, and a safe shelter as well!"

Rapidly he turned toward me. Though the darkness stood between us, there is no doubt that he knew my shape.

"A curse upon you," he said acidly, looking away.

I burned with shyness and shame—though he did not bat an eye. I had sold my most precious possession for nothing. I had accepted degradation, while he displayed only contempt for me.

At next nightfall, I returned to Virgo Star Alley. No sooner had she received me, reclining on her divan, then she called out to me, "Failure is written clearly on your face!"

"We must find another means," I said, sagging forward in my chair in despair.

When I recounted to her what happened, she chuckled sardonically.

"What a mule you are," she berated me. "You approached His Honor in such distinguished attire?"

"What else could I have done?" I answered exasperatedly.

"Perhaps he thought you were one of his rivals, trying to trip him up!"

"In any case, that only confirms that we have to find another way."

"There *is* no other way," she insisted sternly. "You must correct your technique."

I stared in disbelief at her comely face.

"You should wear the proper dress for your task," she declared.

I went home angry with her, as well as with myself, and my demanding desire for security. Days passed while I was absorbed in a mad dialogue with my own mind, until I found myself clad in a *gallabiya* and skullcap, worn-out sandals on my feet, waiting at the same place in the Garden Passage once more. So abased did I feel that it became easy for me—and I no longer let it bother me. When the time came, the man loomed before me with his imposing height. I paused until he was parallel with me, then leapt into action, saying, "I have something for which the eye longs, and for which the soul lusts."

He raised his walking stick at me till I retreated in fright. Then he asked with scornful irony, "What did you say, Your Majesty?"

I fled again to my home, rebuking my disordered self, immersed in the depths of my accumulated angst. As my resentment redoubled, so did my will to succeed as well. I went to the lady and defiantly told her my story. Though shaking her head in regret, she said, "You really are a mule—you need someone to lead you every step of the way."

"I slunk up to him just as any derelict would do!"

"And your voice?" she taunted.

"My voice?"

"Did you talk down to him in the same manner you use with your underlings?"

"I don't think so," I said with evident misgivings.

"Don't waste time," she interrupted. "I'm an expert in these affairs!"

I disappeared for some days, which I spent in anguished contemplation, practicing without any thought of ever giving up. How could I stop trying, when I had sold everything for nothing? When I again took my position in the Garden Passage, patience had depleted me, as well as worry and pain. But then the expected moment came, and I stepped forward nimbly. Lowering my head in humility, I blurted dejectedly, yet with a bitterness that I could not disguise completely, "I have something good for you—in a secure, respectable dwelling."

He kept on going without acknowledging me. Once again I tried to make him hear me.

"You make it sound like a funeral," he rebuffed me.

Promptly grasping my blunder, I became enraged at myself for the excessive resentment that had showed in my voice. I confessed everything to the lady, only to endure her ridicule.

"I will not try again," I said resignedly.

"Have you given up—haven't you even an inch of patience left?"

"The errors are endless," I snorted. "I've had enough."

"Think it over for a while, my old friend," she said in a heartening tone, carefully avoiding any hint of condescension. "How can you consider yielding to despair when you are so close to succeeding? You imagine that you have used up all your forbearance, but what does forbearance cost compared to your ultimate satisfaction? You had a strong start, and no one can say that you haven't made good progress so far. Don't forget that, in the end, you're trying to catch just one man—and not just *any* man."

"He doesn't seem like the kind who would welcome that to me," I said skeptically.

"But that's just the kind he is!" she laughed, then continued more soberly, "If I weren't sure of what I'm saying, then I wouldn't have urged you to make this effort. I'm not one of those who would betray bread and salt."

I left her with my spirit revived, the rose once again blooming in my breast. I waited patiently for days, with no other interest but the Garden Passage, until I found myself again at my accustomed station. As I observed him coming with his sublime stature, I waited until he passed directly in front of me. Then I trailed him abjectly, mumbling, "Don't let the chance of a lifetime elude you!"

When he paid no attention to me, I dogged him obstinately, whining to him softly, "A safe house truly, appropriate for Your Excellency!"

"Where?" he asked abruptly.

With a pleasure I had never before felt in my life, I told him, "In Virgo Star Alley, the third house on the right within."

When we came close to the square he called out to his driver. As the man scurried up to him, he ordered him loudly, "Hold this creep, and get the police!"

Desperately, I thrust the palm of my hand over the driver's mouth. "No—wait—I'm not one of *them*!" I implored him. "I'm a respected person!" I panted, my heart racing.

"Respected?"

"Here's my identification," I said, still gasping for breath.

He turned the card over, studying it carefully. "You look like an imposter," he judged.

I plunged headlong into telling him my story with perfect candor, from the time when my need for security made me first beg for it politely—putting all the other demands of life into it—until that day. The driver remained silent, scrutinizing me in the rays of light falling from a lamp in the square.

"Don't ever show me your face again," he commanded coldly.

After countless days had passed, I dragged my way back to Virgo Star Alley, as though I were now many years older. As I came within sight of the house's entrance, an ancient hag hovered in the currents of darkness, blocking my path.

"The lady is in seclusion," she rasped in a time-ravaged voice.

I knew the owner of this voice, and asked her, "What have you brought me, Mother of Blessings?"

She knew my voice too, and replied, "The lady requests that you avoid all excess, and wait until you are summoned."

My heart leapt as I pressed her, "Is the lady expecting an important visitor?"

"I have no knowledge of anything," she said. "May peace be your companion."

I found no choice but to return. The clouds of obscurity had been raised from hope. She would not have taken this decision if she did not anticipate an auspicious visitation. And why else would she have said, "Wait until you are summoned," if it bore no relation to my conundrum? The veil of darkness is withdrawn from my dream. My heart pounds with visions. Security beams at me with its luminous face through the last deepening shadows of descending night. There is nothing left but to adorn myself with patience—which yearning turns into genuine torture. The days roll on, as the torment of forbearance erupts ever more fiercely, growing ever more rapacious as time goes by. My sole worry is to remain at the ready.

And all the while, but one question keeps recurring to me: *When will the Messenger come?*

Forgetfulness

My searing imagination, its waves exploding in all directions, could never have conjured the endless city, sprawling as far as the eye can see. It was like a disorderly giant of infinite size, waving its thousands of limbs and appendages. Over it towered innumerable rows of massive buildings in the haughty, arrogant style of the age. Another kind, their colors fading, were clearly in the violent grip of time, while a third type was about to collapse in destruction, their residents hanging on in desperate resignation. In every quarter, the people brawled in an uproar, confronting each other in heedless tumult. Busses, cars, horse carriages, camels, and handcarts all followed each other, their noises clashing amidst the countless accidents, blaring weddings, shrieking funerals, bloody arguments, warm embraces, and throats hawking merchandise in the east and west, south and north, the groans of complaint blending with the soft cries of praise and contentment.

The communal home of the immigrants from our village was like a life vest in a stormy sea. The shaykh of the re-settled tribe received me, saying, "Our new son—welcome to your family."

"Thank you, uncle," I said, kissing his hand.

I found my seat at the institute waiting for me too. I was well-thought of, so the trip was crowned with success. I took a post in the government's Survey Department, mus-ing, "Hard work has its reward." And after work I would slip off to the café to see my friends there, though I feared to spend like the other patrons did. My mind was filled with fantasies the way a fasting man dreams of food and drink—for in our residence there were many young flowers just beginning to bloom.

As the wheel of mornings, afternoons, and evenings kept revolving, something unremarkable occurred—a fleeting dream that one either remembers or ignores. Yet it must have shown in my expression, in a way that did not es-cape the attention of our sharp-eyed shaykh. As he sat cross-legged on his couch, mumbling the prayers of his rosary, he said to me, "Something is distracting you."

"A man has come to me in a dream," I confided. "He warned me against forgetfulness."

The shaykh thought for a while, then declared, "He's reminding you not to waste your youth."

I considered carefully what he was saying. In our abode of urban exile, no obstacles were placed between a man and his heart's desires—ours was a compassionate, brotherly tribe. A room was as suitable for a couple as it was for a single person. The bride was already waiting—and there were many kindly acts and favors to help ease the way.

"Let's stick to our holy traditions—with the blessings of God," said the shaykh.

The room was freshly painted and aptly furnished, as well. And so that city which pays no mind to anyone welcomed the new bride and bridegroom. Life in our home away from home was anchored in solidarity; many means were devised to triumph over the hardships of the times. Overwhelmed with happiness, I said to myself, "Our path was paved for us by so many glorious forebears."

Engrossed in love and marriage, in fatherhood and work, one day I told the shaykh, "This is all thanks to God—and to you."

"Our house is like Noah's ark," he answered benignly, "in the raging flood that engulfs us all."

"Uncle," I said, "people have the evil eye for us—they envy us."

"That only grows greater as time goes by," he replied.

I awoke one night with a start at the return of my dream. The same man warned me against forgetfulness. I saw him just as he appeared the first time, or so it seemed. The man was the same man, and the words were the same words.

The shaykh listened with concern. "We have grown used to you dreaming about your fears," he concluded.

"I am quite confident. I have no fears."

"Really?" he queried me. "You aren't concerned for the future of your family?"

"Happy today are those who prepare for their last day," I blurted in protest.

"What would you do tomorrow if the demands of this life should increase upon you?" he asked.

I paused in silent embarrassment.

"Do what many others are doing," he counseled. "Take an extra job."

Through his influence, I was able to start training in a center for plumbing skills. I excelled in a most praiseworthy way—and began to invest my new experience in it in the evenings after I finished my government toil each day. My profits kept growing, and my savings as well. The shaykh watched my success with satisfaction.

"This is surely better than illicit gain," he said. "These days require us to be like the cat with seven lives!"

A marvelous energy pervaded my limbs. I fell rapturously in love with life, disregarding its beating chaos all around us. All this prompted me to lease an apartment for which I paid a sizeable deposit. Inviting me for breakfast, my uncle told me, "This is how things are going these days."

I believed there was no security for any living being without work and money—and the most fortuitous thing that we gain in our world is a dependable future. I maintained my moderation as best I could; the only new things in my life were cigarettes, fatty meats, and oriental sweets. My sons and daughters graduated from foreign language schools, and with the passing days only the best things came to me. Amidst all this delicious abundance, one night my dream returned for the third time. The man warned me against forgetfulness, as he had before. I saw him just as I did the two previous times, or so it seemed: the man was the same man, and the words were the same words.

Astonished, I did not take it lightly. Unfortunately, the shaykh was not at hand to discuss it with me. Being so absorbed in business, I had stopped seeing him briefly, while I hated to visit him for any purpose other than just to say hello. Still, a feeling of unease assailed me, pervading all I did.

Suffering from it harshly, my wife scolded me, "Goodness comes from God, and evil from ourselves."

"What is it but a dream?" I said to her dismissively.

"I don't see you forgetting anything," she replied.

Yet I could not escape the hold of the amazing vision upon me. It was always chasing me, occupying my mind. Under its sway, I rushed from the sidewalk to cross the street, without paying attention to the traffic going by. Suddenly, without any warning, I found myself in front of a car that could not brake in time. Striking me, it threw me through the air like a ball. I lost consciousness completely, until I awoke in the hospital, where I learned there was no hope for my recovery at all.

———

Looking back with pity and sadness, the shaykh later told us:

He was taken to hospital under the dark clouds of

death. There he underwent a desperate operation, while the investigation and the testimony of the eyewitnesses all confirmed that he had run into the road as if wanting to end his own life. The car's driver, therefore, was innocent of any fault. I sat next to my nephew's bed, knowing there was no chance that he would survive, when the driver arrived in humble consolation, offering to render what assistance he could. He stayed for a while, then left on his own.

When he had gone, my nephew's eyelids fluttered, and I saw a familiar look on his face. I bent my head down close to his mouth.

"That's the man," he muttered faintly, "the man in the dream!"

Those were the last words ever to leave his lips.

Beyond the Clouds

I fight my way through life—and it fights back. It's the same way today that it will be tomorrow. From the boons of fortune, all I've gained has been the making of a family and the begetting of children. Then, as I've grown too weak to make them happy, I can no longer make myself happy either. If my own agony was not so uniquely like that of my country, then I would think only of myself, and not of my country. Instead, I have found that my family reflects totally the situation in the country, and that the country exactly mirrors the condition of my family. Both of them suffer from overpopulation, a shortage of resources, an imbalance between income and expenses, ever-increasing debt, and a bleak future. Yet I've never sought to hide the reality of our situation, nor promised to do anything beyond my power to perform. Due to my inability to improve my own condition, along with my impotence to help the nation generally, frustration has turned my hair white before its time. I have found nothing to help me escape into the solace of solitude except for one thing—dreaming.

Yes, dreaming is what hews a new path for me; it brings me all I could possibly crave. With the fullness of health, strength, and human intimacy, dreaming lifts me up to a new world entirely—one of exalted truth and perfect justice. Through dreaming I climb dazzlingly into the world of the Unseen. But sometime during the heat of battle between fact and imagination, the night of misery lengthened as I huddled beneath the bedcovers, all of my limbs trembling uncontrollably. My wife became worried, urging me to take more than one prescription of medicine. Still I longed for sleep, with all its powers to save me from distress and torment. Yet I could neither sleep nor ease the growing agitation that shook me so profoundly. Then, a surprise—and what a surprise! I rose like a bird, flying with calmness and dignity through the air of the room. I could not help thinking of all that I had heard about delirium and fever. I looked and saw my body prone on the bed; all were watching it with streaming tears. This had to be a fever, no doubt about that. All the motion and sounds that surged through the room had no meaning at all to me. I urged them to take hold of themselves, to calm down and keep quiet—but they did not hear. I observed them with complete placidity. Then my interest in them and what they were doing began to decline, and slowly, slowly to disappear. Their image began to sink into the depths, fading away until it had vanished completely. A long corridor stretched before me, whose floor and walls were covered in mist, and from whose distant end loomed the purest light. I walked through it with heavy, stumbling steps, staggering at times, longing for some sense of security. Finally, at the source of the light, my father and mother appeared to me. They stared at me with affection as I rushed toward them, my fears diminishing. Then I remembered the hurdle of death that stood between us. I halted in caution, whispering to them as though in excuse, "Maybe I'm dreaming!"

I heard their two voices as though they were one, "But now you are waking."

They came toward me, arm in arm, wearing clothes made of clouds.

"Wake up! You have become one of us, with nothing standing between us."

Dreams don't have this kind of clarity, I said to myself. Then I whispered, "Yes, I'm completely awake."

"That is good," they replied.

"Yet I feel that a dreadful nightmare is going on inside me."

"That will disperse once you have purged yourself of your sins."

"You will help me . . . ," I said wishfully.

They answered as one, "Our mission here has ended. Rely upon yourself."

In a flashing instant, they were gone. No sooner had they disappeared, than I found myself in my new world.

A new world indeed, which I have not the words to describe. A place, and yet not a place. Light, but yet not really light. Colors, yet not like any that I had known. Trees, but not actual trees. Houses that were not houses at all. Ground and sky shrouded in clouds, spreading outward without any bounds. Even the houses were made of clouds, ranged in even rows with vast spaces between them. The trees towered very high, resplendent in wholly unfamiliar shades of a deeply stirring kind. A steady, soothing light—neither dusk nor twilight—pervaded all. For a moment I imagined that I was alone in an existence that had no clear end. Yet the feeling of loneliness did not weigh heavily upon me, nor did it last long. For this existence that surrounded me was itself pulsing with hidden life. It was also alive and intelligent, regarding me with interest, as though wondering what I was going to do next. And within the homes were living beings absorbed in their own affairs. Their cries of "Glory to God" somehow reached my inner sense of hearing. Should I knock on one of those doors to ask for guidance from those inside? Yet, if even my own parents had abandoned me, then what could I expect from strangers? But where could I start, and where would I go?

Then I was met by a majestic personage whose garment trailed away as a cloud. He gazed at me with his luminous face, a miracle of radiance and beauty. With the look in his eyes, he commanded me to follow him until he stopped before a house.

"This is your dwelling," he said.

I looked at the place as though to inspect it.

"Wait," he warned, "you will not go inside until you have bathed."

I pointed to my heart. "A nightmare is churning above my chest," I told him.

"That is why you must bathe first," he replied.

A disturbing idea flared within me. "It seems that an unceasing labor lies before me," I fretted.

"The road is long, with many stations along the way," he warned. "And its final end is unlike anything else."

"Will you show me how to proceed, at least for the first step?"

"Rely on yourself, both first and last," he bid me.

He took me by the hand and led me through a lush forest to a lake of light, and told me to immerse myself within its waves of rays. I complied with the order—floating for a few seconds, before beginning to sink, slowly and without pause, until I settled in the innermost depths of the lake. The waves penetrated deep inside my being, cleansing me thoroughly. A chain of sins and errors that I had committed during my life stretched out before my sight. Each time a sin or error would vanish, an accompanying pain would vanish with it. My weight lessened accordingly, so that I rose from my submersion little by little. This bathing went on for hours, or days, or years, until eventually I was floating once more upon the lake's surface. Finally, I alighted on the land with nimbleness and glee—then entered my house.

Donning my robe of trailing clouds, I decided not to waste my time in idleness. For a long while I pondered what to do, until finally I resolved to begin with science to meet the needs of the traveler, in mastering navigation and the drawing of maps.

I threw myself into my work with a determination that knew neither weakness nor hesitation. I was aided by the unvarying climate, which was always mild, both by day and by night, not altering even with the seasons. There were no problems to sap one's will, nor any hardships or despair. And from somewhere deep inside me, without any outside help, I had a vision of the great road ahead in all its daunting length and the many stops along its course. My heart was satisfied by the choice of mapmaking as my first field of toil, my elation rising to the enormous heights that I had conjured in my earthly dreams themselves.

But then someone knocked at my door—interrupting my work. Amazed, I told the visitor to enter. Then she—*she*—drew toward me with all her former magic and beauty, swathed in her new, celestial garb. Opening my arms wide, I clutched her to my breast in longing and desire.

"I thought that we would never meet again!" I blurted.

With her sweet voice, she replied, "And I don't believe that, after this moment, we shall ever part again."

"Together, together—until the Abode of Adoration," I said with breathless passion.

Catching sight of my work, she asked, "With what did you begin?"

"With cartography!"

"I started with poetry," she said, with obvious unease.

We exchanged expectant looks, then I muttered, "We cannot stay together."

"Shall we separate by our own choice now," she said, "after we've tasted the bitterness of our ancient parting?"

"We shall not meet again before we arrive at the Mansion of Love."

"That is a long way away."

"Yet we shall get there someday."

"Can't we do anything to help make it come true?"

"I can only do the work which is fitting for me, and perhaps it's the same for you."

"Yes," she replied.

"My desire is the same as yours, or even stronger—yet we have no choice."

She sank into silence. In grief and regret, I told her, "In any case, our reunion is coming—there is no doubt about that. And time has no meaning to us."

She smiled painfully as she receded slowly, until finally she had vanished completely. This time I did not surrender to mourning, as I had in my former existence.

Wary that anxiety might distract me, I redoubled my efforts at work and my enthusiasm for it. Neither the length of the road nor any problems bothered me. Nor did I fear the betrayals of time, or the creep of old age, or the threat of death. Then came yet more knocking at my door. My heart beating hard, I expected to see her beloved face—but this time it was a man, someone new, not the guide who had brought me to my home.

"I am the medium between this world and the one you have left," he said, presenting himself to me.

The old world that I had forgotten utterly. I stared at him questioningly, and he continued matter-of-factly, "I have disrupted your labor, but I am faithful to my duty."

Then he added, still neutrally, "There is someone calling to you from the people of the earth."

What do they want? What have I to do with them? How could they not perceive the importance of the work for which our past lives had prepared us?

"Who is calling for me?" I inquired.

"Your son, Ahmad."

"Ah . . . who was still in his mother's womb when I left their world," I recalled.

My heart pounded despite myself, and I asked, "Would you counsel me to answer his call?"

With polite indifference, he replied, "That is not my affair. You must decide on your own."

A conflict erupted within me, yet I quickly surrendered to this catastrophe, the possibility of which had not previously occurred to me. Under the weight of wicked feelings, I mumbled quietly, "I see that I'd best respond to this plea."

Immediately I found myself peering into a closed courtroom immersed in a kind of darkness. Before me were seats arranged in a semi-circle, on which a group of men were sitting. Among them was Ahmad—whom I knew by my inner sight—who had taken his seat on the right. At the same time, I saw my intermediary reposed on a cushion, a transparent curtain separating him from the rest of those present.

"Ahmad," I called to my son softly.

"Father!" he said, leaping up from his seat.

"Yes, I am your father."

With burning curiosity, he asked me, "How are you, father?"

"God be praised," I answered.

"What is life like where you are?"

"We do not have a language in common for me to convey it to you. But everything here is fine."

Sighing, he rejoined, "Life here seems cruel. Nothing good is left to us."

"You yourselves must change that until all of it is good."

"But how, father?"

"The question is yours, and so is the answer," I said. "All live according to their own ambition."

"Yet all are wondering, what is hidden from us tomorrow?"

"God knows tomorrow, but the human being creates it."

"There's no possibility we can count on your aid?"

"I have already rendered it," I replied.

In a plaintive voice, he exclaimed, "They accuse me of loving only myself!"

"You do not know how to love yourself," I told him, feeling the urge to leave.

Faster than lightning, I was back in my house. There, sharp pangs of repentance and remorse assailed me. How could it not upset me that I should be taken from my noble endeavors to be engrossed in the affairs of the world that is gone? Yet what did I know but the somber guide should then regard me again with his shining visage. The agonies of guilt growing stronger, I appealed to him, "I know that I have faltered, but I will make amends for my fault by working even harder!"

He showed no interest in what I said; his untroubled expression remained unchanged. Then he departed just as he had come, without uttering a word. Yet he left behind him a flower, the likes of which I had never before seen: huge in size, with luxuriant leaves and an enchanting color, emitting a fragrance of unprecedented beauty and power. It dawned on me that he could not have left it without a cause—but certainly had meant it as a gift for me.

A serene happiness overwhelmed me, and I mused to myself, *No doubt, my journey—contrary to what had worried me—has won me such favor.*

The Haunted Woods

———

Over and over again they point to it and warn me. "Don't go near the wood," they say. "It's haunted by demons!"

The wood stands at the southern edge of the Desert of the Prophet's Birthday in Abbasiya. From a distance it looks like a many-peaked mountain of gloomy green, three tram stops in length, and nearly as wide. Overhead the sky perhaps is streaked with smoke borne by the breeze from the rubbish tips, where garbage is always burning. Of what kind are these lofty trees, and what is the reason for their presence in this place? Who planted them here, and why? The Desert of the Prophet's Birthday is where all the young people of Abbasiya go to play football, and where a number of amateur teams practice at the same time. When we finish our friendly matches we pull on our *gallabiya*s over our everyday athletic clothes, then return to our neighborhood—skirting the wood on the way.

Childhood gives way to adolescence. New passions are ignited within me, including the love of reading. In my soul there dawns an enlightenment that celebrates all things new and novel, as many old myths are dispelled from my mind. I no longer believe in the demons of the wood—yet I fail to free myself completely of the latent dregs of fear deep down. I often used to withdraw by myself to the desert, especially during the summer vacations, reading, contemplating, and smoking cigarettes, far from any censorious eye. I would gaze at the forest from afar, smiling sarcastically at my memories. Still, I kept my distance. Finally I grew annoyed with my own attitude, and felt driven to challenge it by asking myself, *Isn't it time you discovered the truth about the wood?*

After not a short discussion, I boldly resolved to do something about it. I chose to act in mid-afternoon, in broad daylight, since the night in any case would not be safe. The place where I used to sit was close to the water pumping station, inside which bustled workers and engineers. Once I greeted one of them and asked him about the secret of the wood. He told me it belonged to the station. He said it was planted a long time ago, taking advantage of the abundant water. It did not extend any further, perhaps, due to the annual celebrations of the Prophet's Birthday next door.

"They say," I remarked, "that the wood's filled with *'afarit*—evil spirits."

"The only demons are human beings," he rejoined.

For the first time I made for the wood. I stopped at its edge peering inward, and saw the towering trees in orderly rows, like soldierly battalions, and the weeds blanketing the ground with their ripe, luscious verdure. A canal cut through them widthwise, shimmering streams branching away from it. Once accustomed to everything, I advanced without trepidation. I met no human being, but became intoxicated on the solitude and tranquility. "What a waste," I thought. "So much time lost—may God suffer those who imagine that Paradise is a refuge for demons." At roughly the center of the wood, some laughter reached me—and in truth, my heart shuddered. Yet my dread vanished in seconds—for there was no doubt this laughter came from a descendant of Adam. I inspected my surroundings with care, and in the distance, made out a small band of youths. Just as quickly I realized they were not strangers, but neighbors and colleagues from my school. I went toward them, clearing my throat—and their heads turned in my direction until I greeted them and stopped, smiling. After a silence, one of them said, "Welcome. What fortunate coincidence brought you here?"

"And what brought all of you here?" I asked instead.

"As you see—we chat with one another, or we read, or have serious discussions."

"Have you been doing this for a long time?"

"Not a short time, in any case."

After some hesitation, I ventured, "I'd be pleased to join you, if you wouldn't mind."

"Do you love study and debate?"

"I adore them with all my heart."

"Then you're welcome, if you wish."

From that time on, I began a new life, that perhaps I could call the life of the wood. During the whole summer vacation, I spent two hours at least each day in this circle, as, with the calling of the birds, thoughts and opinions descended from above. The world had changed, changed utterly. This wasn't merely a diversion or a game, or an intellectual exercise for its own sake. Rather, it led to a journey, an adventure—an experience encompassing all things possible. . . .

By habit I sat with my father and mother after supper. We would listen to the phonograph, talking with one another. I had been concealing the secret of the wood, not revealing it to anyone—and my parents were the last persons I ever imagined to tell about it. A very long time ago— I no longer remember just how long—they went to their eternal rest, and were granted everlasting peace. My father does not get excited unless prodded by news of politics, which he relishes to follow and comment upon. One day he concluded his conversation by exclaiming, "How many wonders there are in this country!"

"Wonders without end!" I rushed to affirm.

He fixed me with an inquiring look. "Let me tell you some of the ideas that circulate in our society," I said.

I spoke concisely, with concentration. He listened in confusion. "I seek refuge in God," he shouted. "The people who hold those views aren't humans—they're demons!"

Only then I understood: I had become one of the demons of the haunted wood.

The Vapor of Darkness

I saw myself on a delightful excursion, like those of our earliest times. Seemingly it was a fair day in winter, for the sky was clear and the sun mild. We arrived together at the square, just as we agreed to meet despite death having parted us. In our hands were little bags made of dyed, woven palm leaves, filled with food and drink. Our throats chirped with laughter as we crossed the eastern limits of the square, heading into the desert nearby, to take our ease by the water springs, the date palms, and the henna trees there. As usual, we spent the day in amusing banter and song, until we were all consumed with pleasure. Then, just before sunset, we returned with our bags depleted to the square, the sun slanting down toward the horizon, as waves of coolness washed over us, tenderly and sweetly. We traded waves of farewell, as the dear ones went down the vacant byways to their homes.

Coming from the square, I lingered quietly for some time near my own home, and—due to the paucity of people out and about at the end of the day—found myself evidently alone. Enjoying the sense of satiety, like a wanderer on the roads, I trekked along my everyday route that passed through the square, running between two rows of markets and commercial agencies, plus workshops for handicrafts and manufacturing. From their midst arose a cacophony of customers' voices, the humming of ovens and the pounding of hammers. Their racket and commotion went on without a lull until well after nightfall, the departure of the busses and the settling of the cash in the registers.

This was the street on which I dreamt when growing up, and when I was working—and it made me very happy to roam its parts. But when its end came in sight, I was surprised to see a barricade of stones completely blocking its exit. Confused and angry, I wondered, when did this obstruction appear? Who had made it? And what was the purpose for making it? Looking around, I noticed that at the barrier's right-hand corner a person was sitting behind a desk on which there was only a telephone. When my eyes settled on him, I was nailed where I stood by a terror I had never before beheld. A coarse face with an aspect that defied all imagination was inspecting me closely. In place of the nose was a short trunk like that of an elephant, while one sunken eye stared out of the middle of its forehead. I did a double take in revulsion and asked myself, *Is that human or animal? What kind of beast could it be?* Yet when I saw the people were undisturbed, engrossed in their affairs, I became confused—and focused all my thoughts on getting myself out of this street that I had mistakenly believed led to my house. I found myself once again in the square, as—just by chance— someone was crossing my path. I blocked the road in front of him, pleading for help. I pointed to the blockaded road and asked, "What's happening on this street?"

He stared at me furiously for impeding his way. "Excuse me," he shouted, "but I've no time for idle talk!"

Then he walked around me and disappeared. For my part, I could think of nothing but getting back home— everything else could bide its time. No doubt the journey had made me giddy—perhaps the next road would prove my true path. How surprised my friends would be when I told them what I saw! Then I entered the start of another street. Narrow at first, it lacked any of the features to show it was really my road. Yet even my urgent doubts of my memory's soundness didn't distract me from my course. This one, too, seemed to be empty. True, both sides were lined with little, well-spaced coffeehouses, yet there was hardly anyone on it. From these cafés floated strange, provocative, and disturbing aromas. Those sitting in them did not seem to hear or see, nor to pay attention to anything. Nor did they look in any way bound to life itself. My strides lengthened as I continued to flee with a creeping unease. Yet when I drew close to the end, my feet were nailed where I stood for the second time. A shiver spread through my limbs, and I couldn't believe my eyes—as I watched a troupe of skeletons doing a popular dance. Yes, Death itself was dancing before my sight, without musical accompaniment! Quickly I retreated before I would faint. *What's happening to the world?* I wondered. *How can I, in all this destruction, find the police in order to take refuge with them? I should go to the police station before heading to my house in order to escape this stifling predicament—while there are still no pedestrians in the square.* But then I remembered the cruel lesson I received from the first man, besides the fact that I had no confidence in anything anymore. There was no serious goal left for me but to get back to my home. And here was the third way—so I resolved to try it out, leaving my fate in the hands of God. Regardless, it was a bustling road beating with the breaths of scores of human beings. Perhaps this was, indeed, my true path, from which I had strayed. From it echoed the cries of those hawking every sort of thing to eat and drink. Customers came empty-handed, and left loaded down with paper sacks, plastic bags, and wrappers. Quickly I sensed a glimmer of hope. But what do I see now, O Lord? One of the customers is drying his tears as he leaves. Another is bent over in agony, screaming as though he'd been fatally stung. And another has thrown a flaming ember into his paper sack—and is now sucking his fingers to cool them off. Though tormented by these evil omens, I did not stop—not until I saw, at the end of the way, a meat seller laying out a row of human heads on his tray. I let out a horrific scream. The buyers, alerted to my presence, began to stare at my own head with interest. Then my body took off and I found myself fleeing, not heed-ing anything until I again reached the square. *O God—have I gone mad?* I raved. Nothing remained but to try the fourth road—and this was the last. What could I do if this one, too, betrayed me?

"What's happened to the world?" I called out aloud.

An angry voice shrieked back at me, "You're frightening me—may God never forgive you!"

I looked at the man apologetically, and motioned toward the final road. "I beg your pardon," I entreated, "I'm exhausted and I need someone to go with me."

He stared at me doubtfully. "I'm sorry," he reproved. "Entrust yourself to God."

He turned about menacingly as he moved away from me. There was nothing left but to try my luck on my own. Sunset was descending without any escape. The road wasn't my normal way, but it seemed to lead to civilization. This was a big, exciting street, remarkable for its magnificence and splendor; one could call it the Avenue of the Grand Cafés. The names of its coffeehouses, painted in electric signs, were frank and defiant: Café of the Pickpockets, Café of the Con Men, Café of the Pimps, Exclusive Café of the Bribe. For the first time I smiled—and whatever would be, would be. The important thing was to return to my house, and let the cafés—with their brazen, openly touted shamelessness, and whoever was in them—go to damnation. I kept up my pace, propelled by both worry and hope. For the first time, I glimpsed at the end of the street something that reassured my heart and calmed my imagination. I saw a band of security men led by a fearsome brute—and had no doubt they were about to launch a vigorous attack to clean the place up and put things in order. With exuberance I sputtered, "May God preserve you! Have you heard what's happening on the other streets?"

I was met with a hail of cold, dry looks that warned of malice and woe. In my stunned dismay, I imagined they were getting ready to arrest me. I began to question their real identities, and sped off without stopping—all too aware that there remained for me no new passage to salvation. I reached the square as darkness was spreading—drowning in a quagmire of confusion, without a life preserver. The place was not empty, as it appeared, but its precincts were occupied with numerous spirits, the atmosphere filled with obscure murmurings. Then cries boomed out, clashing and conflicting to the utmost—raging, threatening, and preparing for combat in the jet-black gloom. I felt myself endangered, though I had no weapon beyond my empty bag. From where did all these creatures come? And what do they want? Are they friend or foe? Did they spring from the desert or from the wild, riotous roads? Then the shouts were permeated with sounds of different kinds—songs of debauchery, religious anthems, and military airs. My chest tightened and I was about to smother, as feelings of annihilation, loss, and despair lashed me onward—until, in the climax of my exasperation, I balled up my fist and struck myself on the skull. . . .

———————

Suddenly, in what seemed a miracle, Hell disappeared. It vanished suddenly, not by degrees, as wakefulness fell from its free kingdom in the sky. An enlightened wakefulness, replete with kindness, peace, and serenity, restful and at rest—a happiness exuding sympathy and affection. I peered through the window—and saw the radiant horizon blooming in the garden of the rising sun.

A Man of Awesome Power

―――――

At a certain time, Tayyib al-Mahdi believed that his mission in this world had come to an end. Deeply relaxed, with only minor aches and pains, he would mutter to himself in contentment, "All praise to God, Lord of the Worlds." He had generous health insurance and a more than adequate pension. He lived in an apartment that he owned in Nasr City, which he had won as a reward for many years of service abroad. His four daughters had each gotten married—there was nothing left for him to do but to spend his evenings with his wife, watching television, reading the newspapers, and listening to the radio channel devoted to the Qur'an.

Was it so strange, then, that he thought he had discharged his duties in life in a commendable way? Yet he had no idea what the future had hidden from him, for one night a man of radiant appearance, bathed in light and wrapped in a snow-white robe, came to him in a dream. In a kindly tone, the apparition told him:

From this moment onward, and for as long as God wills, you shall have the power to tell something, Be!—and it will be. Do with it what you please.

When he woke from his sleep, Tayyib pondered the meaning of his dream. But no sooner had he forgotten it, the way one typically does with dreams, than peculiarly it recurred exactly in its entirety on the following night, and for many nights on end, until he felt there was some secret message hidden within it. Wisely, though, he kept it to himself, telling no one about it, not even his companion in life, his wife Haniya. At the same time, he felt infused with physical energy, filled with confidence, inspiration, and joy. And why not? He was a good man; his sins were forgivable ones. Pious and observant, he was a lover of virtue who lived his life—despite his modest status—as though he bore on his shoulders the worries of the world and of people everywhere.

But from the dream's intense, ceaseless pursuit of him, he decided to try out his supposed new power discreetly. One evening as he was watching a discussion on the first channel on television, his wife Haniya busy in the kitchen, he mentally demanded that it switch to the second channel instead. Without any warning, and without him rising from his seat, channel one disappeared, replaced by a foreign film on channel two. Trembling in violent confusion, he was seized by conflicting emotions of fear and elation.

He kept commanding the television to change channels, and ordering the room's chairs to rise in the air, then returning them to their original places, until he was sure of the miracle that had befallen him. He accepted that its significance was beyond his comprehension—yet he saw that his purpose in the world was not yet fulfilled. Indeed, it had not even begun.

He recalled his benevolent dreams for his country and the planet, which had flared and faded in just a few seconds. Now was the time that they all would come true. He would reform reality with his own hands, but without any acclaim or credit to his name. Yet he reckoned that he must heed the inner voice that had accompanied him through his long life, which occupied his mind when awake or asleep. So at the time that he habitually went to the café each day, he got dressed, his awesome new power enfolded within him, and—entrusting himself to God—left the house in his usual way.

As he hailed a taxi to take him to the heart of the city, the driver waved his hand at him in haughty refusal, speeding on his way without paying him further mind. Even though this was hardly the first time such a thing had occurred, Tayyib's irritation now was greater than in the past. He considered for a moment that he could make the driver suffer an accident on the road. *Whoever is granted a power like mine, must use it only for good.* As he said this to himself, his anger nonetheless got the better of him. He stared at the taxi's rear wheels—and both of them exploded suddenly, like a bomb. The driver pulled over, and drumming his palms together in frustration, glanced back and forth at the two shattered tires. "Both at one time!" he exclaimed.

Tayyib felt that he had taught the man a needed lesson, but had it been mistaken for mere coincidence? He walked by the man, casting him a meaningful look and asking, "Can I be of any help?" but his unknowing pupil glared at him, resentful and enraged. When Tayyib reached the bus shelter, he stood beneath it. As the bus pulled up, jammed with humanity, he watched an argument erupt inside between a woman and a man behind her. He couldn't hear what was going on between them, but he studied the dimensions of the conflict carefully. Then the man suddenly slapped the woman's face with shocking impulsiveness. Tayyib was so startled by the incident that he focused all his anger at the offending man's stomach. Stricken by severe cramps, the brute unexpectedly doubled over, moaning and screaming in pain. The bus didn't move until he had been carried outside for an ambulance to fetch him. Meanwhile, more than one voice cried out, "He deserves it! That's what he gets for his bad manners and cheekiness." Tayyib al-Mahdi observed all this with satisfaction, certain that he had done his duty in the best manner possible.

Continuing on his way to the café, he performed memorable services. Spotting a gaping pothole, he filled it. Finding an electrical box hanging dangerously open, he locked it. Tripping on a pile of rubbish, he removed it. Splashed by sewer water flooding an alley, he drained it. All these things together convinced many in the neighborhood that a genuine awakening had struck the nerves of the state—or even had gone beyond mere awakening to an outright renaissance.

He took his seat in the café, to refresh his mind with a cup of coffee. He listened to the radio as an announcer was expounding on promising developments expected in the future. Tayyib al-Mahdi was annoyed: similar prognostications had excited him in the past, though in the end they had produced only frustration. His chest tightening in fury at what the man was saying, he commanded him from afar . . . *Tell us what has already been accomplished— not what has yet to be achieved!* Then he remarked to himself that only sneezing would stop this broadcaster from speaking. Without warning the man sneezed massively, then remained silent. Perhaps he was drying his nose and mouth with a kerchief. Resuming his chat, he abruptly sneezed again, more emphatically than before. After that, he couldn't complete a whole sentence. The sneezes kept waylaying him until he was forced to conclude that an unforeseen illness had seized him. Rather than trying to talk anymore, he instead played a recorded song, "Walk Around and See."

Tayyib was intoxicated with a rapture of happiness and victory. He would purify both aural and visual broadcasting of what was unworthy of their noble goals. He would terminate any talk that displeased him by making the speaker sneeze spontaneously, or emit trilling cries like those made by women at weddings, or flee at the onset of uncontrollable diarrhea. Without any doubt, he would be the trusty popular censor of the dangerous media of mass communication.

At this time he noticed a man called Sulayman Bey al-Hamalawi surrounded by slavish devotees and followers, not far from his own seat in the café. Sulayman's stooges crowded around their benefactor in hypocritical sycophancy, inflating him grossly with arrogance and conceit. The tax authorities counted Sulayman, one of the fat cats of the reforms, among the city's poor. "Wonderful," Tayyib mumbled. "Just wonderful."

Sulayman Bey, go straight to the tax prosecutor's office to repent and say you're sorry, and pay up the millions of pounds you owe. Immediately the man got up and went to his car parked outside. Tayyib rubbed his hands with glee—tomorrow his victim will be the talk of the newspapers, which will make an example of him to awaken people's consciences. And when Sulayman returns to his villa, he will wonder what had befallen him, beating his head against the wall in despair.

He kept applying his stupendous ability the rest of that day and in the days that followed, in all sorts of different places, wherever it seemed suitable. He passed by a maternity hospital, a consumers cooperative, an electrical appliances factory, and so on. A curse and an affliction for some, a mercy for many others. Wherever he went, astonishment and confusion trailed in his wake. Both those he had chastised and those he had blessed would wonder, "How could people change without warning from one extreme to another? What's happening to the world? How can so many problems be set right, without any steps taken to sort them out?"

Meanwhile, Tayyib came to see that he could not make

the best use of his power without proper planning and awareness of need. He obtained guides to the departments of government, factories, and private companies, and took them to the tea garden at the zoo to draw up a comprehensive program for his intervention: the lairs of official bureaucracy, the centers of production and services, the People's Assembly, the prisons and what was said about them, the commercial markets, the press, the political parties, the schools and universities. Each phase must be mapped out slowly and deliberately. Every clamor must be quieted, every deviation must be deterred. And once he is done correcting his country, he will turn with zeal to deal with the world. The mission that shall emerge from it will be manifold and heavy. Yet the power that he possessed was the wonder of the age!

Something caught his eye at the tea garden's entrance. He saw a beautiful woman approaching, to take a seat at the table right next to him. Gorgeous and enticing, she was a perfect replication of his lost youthful dreams. Swept by a surge of delight, Sulayman found his passions aroused in a way that he not known since he first married Haniya, destroying the indifference he had dreaded since he entered old age. The surprise attraction amazed him—truly it was far from ordinary, and hardly appropriate for one preoccupied with such a mountainous burden as his.

She barely noticed him as her large, round eyes wandered over the zoo's green lake, and the ducks floating lazily on it. Does she have any idea that, in a split-second, he could set her head-over-heels at will? He hesitated a moment before sending her a hidden message. Instantly she threw him an answering look, and seemed as though she were about to speak. His desire now ecstasy, he gave way to it in spite of himself.

Would it do any harm to one who wished to repair the world if he also sought to heal himself? And, in one shared smile, he utterly forgot both his faith and his life. He closed his notebook as they stood up together, surrendering to their fate.

Returning to his house one evening, Tayyib came back to his senses: he realized that he had erred. When Haniya remarked he was not in his normal mood, he claimed to her it was only a cold. And though he never thought to repeat his mistake, the pain it caused him would not go away. Worst of all, he was no longer favored with the depthless inner confidence on which he'd been drunk for so long.

He longed to practice his secret power once again. Waiting until Haniya had gone out on an errand, he turned toward the television as he had done so often before.

The channel would not change.

He thought he was going mad. No matter how much he tried, all he met was failure. The miracle was gone—like a dream.

Pleading is pointless. Distress is useless. Regret has no effect. An awesome sadness will haunt Tayyib al-Mahdi until the day of his death.

The Only Man

Allow me to introduce myself. My name is Satan. That alone should do. You've known my story since antiquity. Indeed, my mission's fame burns as brilliantly as the sun that shall surely scorch me on the Day of Judgment.

Yet I am dazed and confused since it has come to me that, despite all claims to the contrary, there yet exists an honorable man in your country. To avoid any misunderstanding, let me say frankly that I can take no credit whatsoever for the flood of evil that now engulfs the earth. Yet I gladly embrace these new, deviant ideas that never even occurred to me in times of old. I have always accepted my fate, which is to struggle to make man stumble, then bide my time to see the result. But the innovations of this generation far surpass those of all who came before it. Since time immemorial, the art of tempting a single man or a woman would totally absorb me as I resorted to my vast repertoire of tricks and sleight of hand in the effort to snare them. Yet now I simply watch as all humanity throws itself madly into the abyss. Whole groups and peoples fall into the pit without a word passing from my lips, without my moving at all. They all sink together into the mire, while I stand back and wait, puzzled and perplexed, drumming palm against palm. How I have wished that *I* was its cause, the man who put it in motion, the one who could boast it was his own!

But what is really going on? From where did all this corruption come?

Once again, I must confess that times have changed. Every day there is some new miracle or wonder in the world. Indeed, I realize that today I must study economics and politics, public speaking and propaganda, and learn all about science and technology, as well as contractors' and agents' commissions, and the ways and means of illegal immigration. I have to become more cultured and change my former ways, if I don't want my cause to be defeated, to lose my very reason for being. Otherwise, my immortal rebellion would vanish fruitlessly into the void, leaving not a trace behind.

I was in this state of frustration and confusion when my spies informed me that there is still a man of integrity left in this land.

"His name is Muhammad Zayn," they told me. "A judge by profession, he lives at 15 Zayn al-Abidin Street."

Immediately I began watching this man with special

care. His residence is an old house, ill-suited to his status. That is where he grew up with his family until it was left to him as one by one his kin passed away. Nonetheless, it is considered a great boon from the Lord in an era when people are living in tents and tombs. He is married, with a son at university and another son and daughter in secondary school. He sets off alone for the bus to the courthouse each day, getting off one stop early so that people do not see him riding amidst the crowd, clutching his briefcase under his arm. He starts his court sessions at the scheduled time, following the testimony of the prosecution, the defense, and the witnesses with startling concentration and concern. Other than that, he hardly ever leaves his home except out of necessity, to study his legal briefs sometimes, or to pay his bills. He instills the spirit of hard work and abstinence in his children, who do not hold themselves above the offspring of paupers. Overall, the household abides in an air of plain modesty—in demeanor, in clothing, and even in food. His wife, though, endures this with resentment, easing her feelings by complaining, and by cursing the age from time to time.

"You have my entire salary in your hands," the judge tells her. "I cannot turn base metals into gold. I do not speculate about the savage cost of living, because I live in the protection of God, who shall preserve me from perdition until my last breath is drawn."

A great man, but blighted just the same. Temptations surround him from all sides, like water and wind. I found the urge of conquest aroused in me, for right before me were his wife and family. What's more, it was a household fully aware of what was going on around it. Here you have a conversation that shows the divisions between a husband and his spouse:

"What kind of world is this?" she asked. "Are we doomed to all this torment simply because we're good?"

He cut her off firmly. "This is the lot of the honest in hellish times."

"They're all thieves, as you know very well!" she declared.

"Yes, they are—they're all thieves."

"And how will it all end?"

"My sole possession is patience," he rejoined.

This display was both an objection to the way things were going, and a reproach to her husband's virtue, as well.

The daughter listens a great deal; she reads the daily papers, and takes time to think about worldly affairs. Shall her marriage take place under these dreadful conditions? I did not shrink from sending her a beguiling young man, as well as a female colleague with know-how in finding furnished flats—yet the young couple stopped at the edge of sin.

"The crooks are safe, playing around as though they're above the law," the daughter declared. "Meanwhile, the law itself is wretched—and is only applied against the wretched."

"All doors are open for their children," said one of Muhammad's own. "Only they have good opportunities."

"All we get is suffering, and honey-coated lies."

"Our father is an honorable man. An honest judge—but weaker than a wealthy criminal!"

I was delighted by what I heard and prepared myself for work. Everything in my existence is done in seconds. My task seemed extremely easy. I decided to leave the man alone to focus on his children. If one wants to subdue a fortress, then he must first look for a weak point in its walls. There is where he must put his toughest toil.

The ecstasy that precedes effort lit up my heart. Soon, though, it was mixed with something, and—O how quickly and strangely!—this something resembled an odor of dubious origin. The euphoria ebbed away like a wave fleeing the shore. I fell into a state of lassitude, a torpor like a sense of being foiled, as though I were ashamed of myself for the first time in my deep-rooted history. I hesitated, when I had never hesitated before. I flinched, when I had never flinched before. Whatever lust I had had for battle, my victory in it was cause for derision, a defeat sure to bring shame.

No, Satan—this is not mere indolence, it is renunciation. I have never had such a contretemps before. I will leave you, Mr. Muhammad, to your blameless travail, to your trying personal circumstances, and your torturous dependents. You are not happy, but still they envy you. You do not succumb to them, so they try to provoke you. No one loves you. No one empathizes with you. They bear a grudge against you and plot ceaselessly to spite you with the worst of wills.

Now I will bid you adieu. I'll follow your news from afar. You shall remain a black stain on my being forever.

If ever I'm asked about you, I will reply, "That man stopped the Devil from doing his job."

The Rose Garden

———

All of it happened such a long time ago. The shaykh of our alley told me the story as we sat one day in a garden full of roses. . . .

Hamza Qandil was found after a long disappearance, a stiffened corpse lying out in the desert. He had been stabbed in the neck with a sharp object. His robe was soaked with hardened blood, his turban strewn down the length of his body. But his watch and his money had not been touched—so clearly robbery had not been the motive. As the authorities began to look into the crime, word of what happened spread through the quarter like a fire through kindling.

Voices rang out from within Hamza's house. The neighbor-women shared in the customary wailing, and people traded knowing looks. An air of tense drama spread out through the *hara*. Yet some felt a secret satisfaction, mixed with a certain sense of guilt. "Uncle" Dakrouri, the milk peddler, expressed some of this when he whispered to the prayer leader of our alley, "This murder went beyond what anyone expected—despite the man's pig-headedness and lack of humor."

"God does what He will," answered the *imam*.

The prosecutor's office asked about the victim's enemies. The question exposed an atmosphere of evasion, as his widow said that she didn't know anything of his relations with the outside world. Not a soul would testify that they had ever seen a sign of enmity between the murdered man and anyone else in the quarter. And yet, no one volunteered any helpful testimony. The detective looked at the shaykh of the *hara* quizzically, saying:

"The only thing I've been able to observe is that he had no friends!"

"He got on people's nerves, but I never bothered to find out why," the shaykh replied.

The investigation revealed that Qandil used to cut through the empty lot outside of our alley on his way to and from work in the square. No one would accompany him either coming or going. When the traditional question was asked—"Did the folks here complain about anyone?"—the consistent response was a curt denial. No one believed anybody else, but that's how things were. But why didn't Hamza Qandil have a single friend in the alley? Wasn't it likely that the place held a grudge against him?

The shaykh of the *hara* said that Qandil had a bit more

learning than his peers. He used to sit in the café telling people about the wonders of the world that he had read about in the newspapers, astounding his listeners, whom he held entranced. As a result, every group he sat in became his forum, in which he took a central place considered unseemly for anyone but local gang bosses or government officials. The neighbors grew annoyed with him, watching him with hearts filled with envy and resentment.

One day, tensions reached their peak when he talked about the cemetery in a way that went far beyond all bounds of reason. "Look at the graveyard," he grumbled. "It takes up the most beautiful place in our district!"

Someone asked him what he wanted there instead.

"Imagine in the northern part houses for people, and in the south, a rose garden!"

The people become angry in a way they had never been before. They hurled reproaches at him in a hail of rebuke, reminding him of the dignity of the dead and the obligation to be faithful to them. Most agitated of all was Bayumi Zalat; he warned him not to say anything more about the cemetery, shouting, "We live in our houses only a few years—but we dwell in our tombs till the Day of Resurrection!"

"Don't people have rights, too?" Qandil asked.

But Zalat cut him off, enraged. "Religion demands respect for the dead!"

With this, Zalat, who didn't know the first thing about his faith, issued his very own religious ruling. But later, after the battle began to cool, the shaykh of the *hara* came, bearing a decree from the governor's office. The order called for the removal of the cemetery by a fixed deadline—and for the people to build new tombs in the heart of the desert.

There was no connection between what Qandil had said and this decision, though some thought there was—while others believed, as the Qur'an says, that it's wrong to suspect someone unless you have proof. Meanwhile, most people said, "Qandil certainly isn't important enough to influence the government—but in any case, is he not like an evil omen?"

All in all, they blamed him for what happened, while, from his side, he made no effort to hide his pleasure at the decree. The people's frustration and anger kept getting stronger and stronger. Finally, they gathered before the shaykh of the *hara*, the men crying out and the women lamenting, and demanded that he tell the authorities that the government's order was void and forbidden: that it was against religion, and fidelity to the dead.

The shaykh replied that his reverence for those who have died was no less than theirs. Nonetheless, they would still be moved, in absolute compliance with the laws of God, and of decency. But the people insisted, "This means that a curse will fall upon the *hara*, and upon all who live there!"

Then the shaykh called out to them that the government's decision was final, and charged them to ready themselves to carry it out. At this, Zalat pulled away from them. In a braying voice, he declared:

"We haven't heard anything like that since the age of the infidels!"

Their anger with the government mixed with their anger at Qandil until it became a single, seething fury. Then, one night, as Bayumi Zalat was returning from an evening out, he took a shortcut through the tombs in the cemetery. There, at the little fountain, a skeleton loomed before him, wrapped in a shroud. Zalat halted, nailed where he stood, while everything that had been in his head instantly flew out of it. Then the skeleton spoke to him:

Woe unto those who forget their Dead, and who neglect the most precious of all their possessions—their graves.

Zalat stumbled back to the *hara*, his heart filled with death's whisperings. And in truth, he didn't conceal from anyone that it was he who had killed Qandil. Yet no one divulged his secret, whether out of fear, or out of loyalty. Gossip said that this fact had even reached the police commissioner himself. But he, too, had been against moving the cemetery in which his ancestors were interred. The blame was laid against a person unknown—and so Hamza Qandil's blood was shed unavenged.

———

The shaykh of the *hara* ended his talk on a note of regret, as we sat in the rose garden that—once upon a time—had been the graveyard of our ancient quarter.

The Reception Hall

———

Today is my birthday. The feast of life renewed. We gather in the grand reception hall and our emotions warm it in the full force of winter. All that is delicious and delightful in food and drink and sweet song surrounds us. We come singly and in couples and in groups. Love guides us forward and good camaraderie binds us together. Differing moods and tempers blend in our hearts. We have no need to hire entertainers, for among us are excellent singers and glorious dancers—and what are these but our joy of life bursting out? Our joking evening banter is completely informal and unrestrained. The fragrance of flowers wafts through the room, which glitters with pleasure and contentment. The soirée stretches on till the coming of dawn, when we go out little by little, the same way we came in, eyelids sagging with satiety, throats hoarsened by laughter and loud talk, as dreams draw us on to happy slumber.

We are decreed from birth to be divided only by the Destroyer of Delights—but he seems quite far away. Security, it appears, is granted us. Of course, our numbers dwindle and faces disappear in the passing of days. The span of life has its dominion, and circumstances have their dominion, and what lasts forever but the One who is eternal? In the flood of pleasure and its warmth, we overlook the losses and savor what is fated for us, but with a deep sense of grief.

"That beautiful, bewitching face!"

"And her girlfriend who would never stop laughing!"

"And that self-important character who made himself the maestro at every party!"

We philosophize and say, "Well, that's life and we must take it as it is. It's been that way since the age of Adam, always treating people in the same fashion. . . . So where's the surprise?"

But the debate subsided as the hall was emptied of its heroes. Today, no one comes, not a man or a woman. I wait and wait in hope that maybe . . . but it's no use. I am tortured by loneliness, as my loneliness is tortured by me. I am unaware of what goes on beyond my sight. Nothing remains but mummified imaginings in the sarcophagi of memory. Sometimes I believe—and sometimes I do not. There was nothing in my heart but bruises and wounds, and affection for that One who dwells within me, when he asked me, "Shall I tell you the truth?"

"Please."

"They have all been arrested," he said. "The Guardian executes his duty, as you are aware."

"But they're all so different. How can he arrest them all without distinguishing between them?"

"He is not concerned with differences."

"Do you foresee when they will be released?" I asked, with intense distress.

"Not one of them shall be freed," he answered, his voice frigid with finality.

Ah! He means what he says. None of them shall be spared. The period of my loneliness shall linger and lengthen. But the matter didn't stop there. Motion is eternal and unceasing. I was watching a moth fluttering about my lamp when he breathed in my ear, "Be warned. . . . They are looking into you."

Really? No matter how long your voyage, your mission keeps growing with it, an old saying goes. But anxiety did not grip me as it did of yore. I listened to him as he whispered, "There is a chance for survival."

I heard without heed. He was goading me toward the impossible. He often teased me this way—but I felt neither fear nor a desire to protest. Nor was I without a certain strange pleasure.

"No," I told him.

And I occupied myself with packing my bag.

I alternate between packing my bag and amusing myself by watching the comings and goings.

I wrap myself in my robe against the cold of winter. I stand behind the windowpane, the glistening earth shaded by the boughs of trees, the sky obliterated by clouds. My eyes observe closely. More than once I spot him as he crosses the road, his tall, slender figure untouched by age. But he has not yet headed toward my house. In my youth I was deceived by his friendship with my father and his praise for him, and then . . . what was the result? That amazing man! During the days when I was deceived with what there was between him and my father, I came upon him unexpectedly on the street near my home. In all innocence, as courtesy demands, I invited him to visit us.

"Not today—thank you, my son," he said, smiling.

How often people are confused by his kind reputation and his sadistic acts! In an interview a woman journalist asked him about his preoccupations.

"That I execute my duty to perfection," he explained.

She pointed out examples of iniquity that sometimes occur.

"My work is carried out with perfect justice!" he rejoined.

"Have you never once loathed your duty?"

"Never—I execute a law that is absolutely just."

"Aren't there incidents that deserve explanation?"

"If we get into these legalistic details, the readers will lose all patience with me!"

And so the reporter ended the interview by noting his complete self-assurance.

Such is the man whose name breathes terror into hearts, who once declared publicly, "I do not go to people to arrest them. Rather, it is they who come to me by themselves."

He added, "Likewise I deny with vehemence all that is said about the torture practiced in prisons."

———

And so, here I am, looking out from behind the window-pane, during the brief moments in which I pause from packing my bag.

A Warning from Afar

We had not thought that Hasabu, who warned us of danger, would ever amount to so much. He used to sell perfumes for a meager profit, though his wealth in human affection knew no bounds. His most prominent qualities were his soundness and reliability. In his leisure time he would dabble in song, loving to stay up late talking, though he didn't partake of a water pipe except behind the neighborhood tombs.

One morning he came back from his late night out, his face white and his mind distracted. He told his friends in the coffeehouse that he had been summoned as he returned in the dark, finding himself surrounded by furious ghosts. He learned from their conversation that they were skeletons of the former residents of our quarter. They were agreed among themselves that what was now going on here was morally forbidden. They asked him to serve as their herald, warning the people of the *hara* that if they didn't put right their affairs, and return to the straightened path, then the spirits would creep upon them as an army of walking bones, cleansing the quarter of both sin and sinners.

Some people laughed. Others cracked jokes. Yet they all fell speechless in view of his intense sadness, and his tearful, dejected looks.

"You're serious, Hasabu!" said one.

"We've never known you to be a liar!" declared another.

"But what you're saying is simply impossible!" opined a third.

So he answered in a quavering voice, "Sublime is His power. . . . He says of something, *Be!*—and it is. . . ."

Amazingly, what Hasabu said greatly affected many souls. One group repeated what is said of the Holy Traditions, that there can be no altering them. Others clung to the word of the All Powerful, who knows no limits. The wise men, common folk, and fools alike became caught up in all this until it kindled civil strife. The shaykh of the alley finally felt compelled to intervene, calling out to them on market day, "What have you to do with these arcane affairs? Have you given up your daily concerns?"

He appealed for help from the prayer leader of the local Sufi order, but the disputation persisted and grew out of control. Insults were traded, and fistfights broke out.

During all this, they would refer to the warning of the

Dead as if it were an undeniable fact. Yet this did nothing to diminish the deviations from the righteous way that took place every day, as though there was no relation between the two.

As for Hasabu, he withdrew from the life of his alley—and was drawn instead to the world of the Unseen with all its force. All connections between himself, people, and material things were cut, as he retired with his white robe, green turban, and cryptic speech. He spent most of his days at the cemetery's edge, staring into the wasteland beyond, awaiting whatever Time would bring.

Arabic Text Sources

"The Seventh Heaven" was published as "al-Sama' al-sabi'a" in *al-Hubb fawq hadabat al-haram*, 1979.

"The Disturbing Occurrences" was published as "al-Hawadith al-muthira" in *al-Hubb fawq hadabat al-haram*, 1979.

"Room No. 12" was published as "al-Hujra raqm 12" in *al-Jarima*, 1973.

"The Garden Passage" was published as "Mamarr al-Bustan" in *al-Tanzim al-sirri*, 1984.

"Forgetfulness" was published as "al-Nisyan" in *al-Tanzim al-sirri*, 1984.

"Beyond the Clouds" was published as "Fawq al-sahab" in *al-Fajr al-kadhib,* 1989.

"The Haunted Wood" was published as "al-Ghaba al-maskuna" in *al-Fajr al-kadhib*, 1989.

"The Vapor of Darkness" was published as "Dukhan al-zalam" in *al-Qarar al-akhir*, 1996.

"A Man of Awesome Power" was published as "al-Rajul al-qawi" in *al-Qarar al-akhir*, 1996.

"The Only Man" was published as "al-Rajul al-wahid" in *al-Qarar al-akhir*, 1996.

"The Rose Garden" was published as "Hadiqat al-ward" in *Sada al-nisyan*, 1999.

"The Reception Hall" was published as "al-Bahw" in *al-Qarar al-akhir*, 1996.

"A Warning from Afar" was published as "Nadhir min ba'id" in *Sada al-nisyan*, 1999.

"Mahfouz is the single most important writer in modern Arabic literature."
—Newsday

VOICES FROM THE OTHER WORLD
Ancient Egyptian Tales

Nobel laureate Naguib Mahfouz reaches back millennia to his homeland's majestic past in this enchanting collection of early tales that brings the world of ancient Egypt face to face with our own times. From the Predynastic Period to the twentieth century, these five stories conduct timeless truths over the course of thousands of years.

Fiction/Short Stories/1-4000-7666-8

THEBES AT WAR

Thebes at War tells of ancient Egypt's defeat of Asiatic foreigners who had dominated northern Egypt for two hundred years. With a visit from a court official and a provocative insult, the southern pharaoh's long-simmering resentment boils over, leading him to commit himself and his heirs to an epic struggle for the throne. *Thebes at War* is a resounding call to remember Egypt's long and noble history.

Fiction/1-4000-7669-2

KHUFU'S WISDOM

At the center of Mahfouz's first novel is the legendary Fourth Dynasty monarch Khufu, for whom the Great Pyramid of Giza was built. When a seer prophesies the end of Khufu's dynasty and the ascension to the throne of Djedefra, son of the High Priest of Ra, the pharaoh must battle to preserve his legacy against the will of the Fates. But in the face of the inexorable attraction between Djedefra and Princess Meresankh, Khufu's beautiful daughter, Khufu must consider not only his personal ambition and the opposing decree of the heavens, but also how the wisdom he prides himself on as a ruler will guide him in determining the fate of his daughter's heart.

Fiction/1-4000-7667-6

RHADOPIS OF NUBIA

While ravishing courtesan Rhadopsis is bathing, a falcon lifts one of her golden sandals and drops it into the lap of the Pharaoh Merenra II. Upon hearing Rhadopsis described as "beauty itself," the young pharaoh decides to return Rhadopsis's sandal himself. When the two meet, they are immediately seized by a passion far stronger than their ability to resist. But blinded by their passion, they ignore the growing resentment of the world around them.

Fiction/1-4000-7668-4

ANCHOR BOOKS

Available at your local bookstore, or call toll-free to order:
1-800-793-2665 (credit cards only).